THE
NINTH
FACTION

Leslie Rosoff and Zoë Gilbertson

FRESH INK

an imprint of

SOCIETY OF YOUNG INKLINGS

The Ninth Faction

Copyright © 2021 Leslie Rosoff and Zoë Gilbertson

Requests for information should be addressed to:

Society of Young Inklings, PO Box 26914, San Jose, CA 95126.

Cover Illustration: Safiya Shahjahan

Interior Design and Composition: Naomi Kinsman

Printed in the USA

First Printing: August 2021

ISBN: 978-1-956380-06-4

To our parents, for helping us pursue our dream of writing,
as well as funding our mentorships.

And to Ms. Carolina Smit, for inspiring us to keep writing.

CONTENTS

PROLOGUE

It was a dark, starless night. A soft blanket of snow covered the ground. It was a new moon that night, but even a full moon would be smothered by the countless storm clouds that would produce yet another layer of snow.

A woman and her husband walked through the woods, seeking shelter from the coming blizzard. When they found a place to stop, the woman opened up a basket and pulled out two small bundles.

"Can I see them? It's been days since their birth, and I am becoming worried. Are they all right?" the man asked, his voice almost drowned out by the wind.

The woman bit her lip, but reluctantly unwrapped the tiny bundles. Beneath the warm cotton blankets she revealed one baby in each bundle. One had two grey pointy ears and a fluffy tail, and the other had small feathered wings and sharp claws instead of fingernails. The man looked at his wife in dismay. Although he said nothing, from the look on his face and the fear in his eyes anyone could tell he was furious. More than that, he was scared. A Fantastical child only meant danger—danger that was controlled by magic, magic that wasn't even controllable itself.

"If they are Fantasticals, then that means you are too," the man said harshly.

The woman took her hooded cloak off to reveal a short, golden horn between two pointy ears. She had a beautiful tail with pinks and blues and yellows that all flowed together like a rainbow after a storm.

"You've been hiding this from me!" the man shrieked.

The Fantastical said nothing.

The man, wide-eyed, buttoned his cloak and ran off into the night. A silent tear trickled down the Fantastical's face. She didn't follow, instead remaining right where she was. She looked down at her children sadly. After a moment, she wrapped them up safely again and raced through the wilderness. She stopped in a circle of trees and put the basket down.

"Aikai, I know you can hear me."

A pair of amber eyes stared down from the dark canopy above. They seemed to be watching, or perhaps *waiting* for something to happen.

"You owe me a favor... I understand this may be a larger one, but I really need your help. I was discovered, and now they are coming. Please, watch over my children until they are ready. I put a spell on them that will hide their powers and features, but it will not last forever. Magic chooses all, remember that. Goodbye... You will not see me again."

PERIL FOREST

EILSEL PAWZORD

I live in a haunted forest.

Joking, it's not really haunted. It's called Peril Forest, and it's supposedly home to devilish horses with horns. I've never actually seen one, so I'm pretty sure they don't really exist.

Aikai says they do, though. He says that one saved the whole forest, but when I asked how he just looked sad. He doesn't do that very often, though. I wonder if he believes what the outside world says: 'unicorns,' as they're called, steal people's life essence or something. I saw a poster that must have come from one of the neighboring villages with that warning written on it. Honestly, though, I doubt Aikai thinks that. He believes that almost any creature can do good. If a unicorn saved the forest, Aikai probably likes them even more than other creatures. However, unicorns are nearly extinct, so it doesn't matter much. The last one was spotted almost twelve years ago now, around the time my twin and I were born. Anyway, Aikai's a great dad, for an owl.

Aikai isn't a true owl. He looks like a normal human... except for the fact that his hair is made of feathers, his eyes are amber, and he can turn his head around in a way that creeps me out every time. But other than that, he wears glasses and has light brown skin. However, his skin gets darker around his face, sort of like a mask. I've seen actual owls like that, so it makes sense.

Oh, I forgot! He has *wings*! Actual, feathery wings. Those are pretty cool, but when Aikai's not flying, his wings are usually tucked behind his back. Eoz is always asking Aikai about what it's like to have wings. She's always saying that she'd really like to have them. I don't wonder as much—heights are not my friend. Anyway, Aikai's great, and he's like a dad-teacher type of guy.

I know he's not my real father, because he's an owl and my sister and I are human. Fine, fine, he's not really an owl. He's something called an Aviaren, which are people with bird-like features. For example, wings, larger eyes, feathers. There are other kinds of animal-humans, and they can also be referred to as humanoids. There are Prowls, Scalians, Bouldax, etc. But there's one type that's almost never talked about, and

Aikai acts super weird whenever they're brought up. The ninth faction–
the Fantasticals. Those humanoids have true magic, and their features
are drawn from mystical creatures, such as unicorns. I asked Betty about
them once, and in a hushed voice she whispered that they were very
dangerous. She was probably just trying to scare me, though. I think the
Fantasticals are super cool, but all the history books say they're extinct.
Aikai once said they weren't, but afterwards he never mentioned the topic
again.

Then there's my sister. Everyone's always surprised when we say
we're twins, and then they usually cite the same reason *every time* as to
why they think so: "You don't look alike."

And it's true, we don't look alike. My eyes are blue, hers are green.
My hair is a lighter brown, hers is almost black.

I hear footsteps coming from Aikai's room, which is near the living
room space that I'm in right now. The sofa that I'm sitting on is dark red
and in front of it is a stone fireplace. A rug covers most of the floor. To
the back of the room is a table that we rarely ever use, as we usually sit
outside to eat. The room itself is made with boards that give it a nice, log-
cabin feel, and various bookshelves adorn the walls. Then, there's also a
somewhat embarrassing painting that Eoz and I made when we were little.

Before I was allowed to hunt, Eoz and I would run around the
forest looking for flowers. One day, when we brought them back, Aikai
smashed them. We were horrified—until we realized that he had made

paint! We used sticks with leaves tied to their points to smear the paint on a piece of paper. In the end, there was a horrible stick-figure drawing of me, Eoz, and Aikai. I always laugh when I see it. It reminds me of times when fewer soldiers patrolled our woods.

For some reason, troops of Auroran soldiers sometimes come here from time to time. Aikai says that most of the Aurorans think that the forest is haunted, which is as stupid as calling Aikai a Prowl. The worst thing I've seen in here, beside the Demon-Bear, are the soldiers themselves!

I walk outside. In the middle of the balcony, a circle of stones is lined with sticks that lean against each other. At night, Aikai grabs whatever animal I've hunted, plus any plants Eoz has gathered, and carries them up to the balcony by the sticks. Then, we light the sticks on fire, and put the foodstuff in a cauldron of sorts. Don't worry—we're not witches! Anyway, the fire would probably be a problem inside the treehouse, but the balcony has never burned—even though it's made of wood. Whenever we ask why, Aikai always tells us it's magic.

Speaking of Aikai, I hear him calling now. "Eilsel! Your part of the room is a mess, could you please go clean it?"

I slouch a bit from where I'm sitting on the sofa. The room is definitely a mess, but I can't really help it. Aikai says I probably could, pointing out that I'm only reading, hunting, or really just doing anything to get out of cleaning.

"Uhh, maybe I should go hunting?" I say, trying to sneak away from my messy domain.

"Eilsel, I've let you get away with not cleaning it for a while now, but it's almost as bad as when you were eight."

I don't think the room is that bad. When I was eight, stuff had been everywhere. And I mean *everywhere*. Cloaks had slipped from hangers, arrows poked out from my hunting bag, and a broken carving knife cluttered the floor.

Aikai had finally cracked down on me, and I spent a whole day cleaning my side of the room. By the time I was done, it looked a lot better compared to how it had been. It was still a mess, though. I never really got around to totally fixing it.

"If it's that bad, I'll go clean it. Sorry, Aikai." I frown as I say this.

"It's fine, Eilsel. But now you have to go clean it." He chuckles. "I can't let you get out of it."

I venture to the side of the treehouse opposite where we eat and grab the old tree that has grown up to our window. The tree always been there, and for as long as I can remember, Eoz and I have used it to get up to and down from our room. I place a foot on a branch that protrudes out from the trunk and haul myself up to a higher section of the tree.

Once I'm high enough, I turn around and look through the window. A small ledge extends from it. The ledge is made of birch wood, unlike the rest of the treehouse, which is mostly an old oak. We usually pull the ledge up at night, and also when it's raining, but we lower it down in the daytime. We use it to make the leap to the tree easier. I jump across and glance around the room.

Sure enough, my side of the room is a total disaster. It looks even worse than it actually is, because Eoz's part of the room is a perfect masterpiece. It's all clean and everything is in its place.

"Well, this is gonna take forever." I sigh.

"You know, if you cleaned it earlier it wouldn't be this bad," Eoz tells me.

"Yeah, I know," I reply.

"I could probably help you if you want," Eoz says and smiles. "If you were to keep it clean."

Uh-oh, I am not sure I can do that. But... I do want it clean now, so I'll agree and hope she forgets later.

"Yeah, okay. I'll try," I say.

Eoz crosses over to my side of the room. "Okay, first things first, you need to take everything out."

She starts piling my stuff in the middle of the room. I don't know why Eoz is moving every single item, but I do know that she organizes her stuff much more than I do, so I don't say anything.

I try to help, but apparently Eoz has some kind of sorting system that I don't know, so she tells me to go 'look around the room.' Eoz's part of the room is painted mint green, which she now thinks is a tad babyish. My half of the room goes well with Eoz's; it's a light blue that is reminiscent of my favorite color.

Eoz's side has two bookshelves, from which I commonly steal reading material, much to her annoyance. Especially since I often forget to give her books back. Her bed is right in the middle of her section. There are curtains all around the bed, and it's backed up against the wall. Eoz also has a little desk with a chair nearby.

Then there's my domain. Unlike Eoz, my bed is raised above the ground, so there's something like a cave space underneath it. That's where I hide all the books I've taken from Eoz's bookshelves. Technically, they're supposed to be both of our books, but Eoz has taken it upon herself to be their caretaker. I believe this is somewhat unfair, so I have been steadily building up my collection. I'm pretty sure she's noticed though.

Ehh, anyway, one of Eoz's favorites that I could never take, is *The Knights of Magic*. It's about this kid named Ezra who leaves his home to become a knight, or something like that. Eoz is all about adventure, so it only makes sense that she would enjoy books of that genre.

I like to read about the history of this world, too. There's a lot of interesting stuff to learn, as long as you're able to disregard the obvious dislike of humanoids in most books with human authors. It's difficult to do that, though, so I stick to novels with non-biased human authors or humanoid ones. I was surprised at first to learn about how the Demon-Animals, such as Demon-Monkeys, and of course, the dreaded Demon-Bears, are descendants of normal humanoids. In fact, some are so old that they were actually humanoids, not just descendants. However, instead of becoming normal animals when they died, like other humanoids, they became Demon ones. Some think that it was because they were cursed, yet still others believe that they had committed unimaginable—terrible—deeds. No one really knows, though.

"Eilsel! I finished piling your stuff. There was a *lot* of it! Now, you have to put it away."

"But Eoz, I'm never gonna get this done!" I groan.

She shrugs. "Sorry Eilsel, but it's your mess."

With that, she drops through the window, heading to the floor below. I look at the mess before me. I imagine myself cleaning it up and sigh. That's never gonna happen, and if it somehow does, I'll probably trip over a book and knock myself out. Then I would freak everyone out. I would never want to worry my sister and Aikai, though sadly I've done it many times before. After they freaked out and I woke up, I would have to explain why I had been knocked out, which would be oh so very fun.

I pick up my hunting equipment and pack it into a bag that I can sling over my shoulder, then put it down by my bed-cave-thing. Then, I go back to the pile and grab the hunting stuff I won't be using and hang it up in the closet.

I really, really don't want to be cleaning my room right now. I could be hunting outside or even spying on Owl-Kids with Eoz. *Anything* but this, really. I sigh because I know there's no way I'm getting out of it.

I realize that Eoz found the books I had taken, so I frantically shove them into a bag and then carry them back into my cave. I place them in a bin under the bed. After that, I store my clothes inside a bin and put on my second favorite blue tunic. I want to save my absolute favorite one for my birthday.

After an hour of putting things away, I'm finished. I walk towards my cave and... *trip over a book*, hitting my head on the wall, knocking myself out.

When I wake up, two faces stare down at me. Oh, no. I hit my head hard enough to faint? And of course, there are Aikai and Eoz, who are probably worried as a Bouldax who has lost their tools. I sigh.

Wow. Just wow. The irony stings, doesn't it?

HUNTING GROUNDS

EOZ PAWZORD

"Bullseye!" Eilsel shouts as her arrow shoots straight into a fox's rib. The fox whimpers and blood drips from its side.

I roll my eyes. "I don't understand why you make me come with you. You know I hate standing out here all day."

Eilsel eyes the bronze fox, trying to find a way to get the creature home. Despite its average size, it looks quite heavy.

"You see, when I hunt I like to be with someone." She pauses. "The same way you like me to come when you spy on the other owls."

That's true. I do like it when Eilsel comes with me to spy on the other owls, but Eilsel is so clumsy that we always get caught.

"So, umm, will you help me carry it back?" Eilsel asks timidly.

How is that even a question?

"Of course not!"

I try to recall a time when I willingly carried a dead animal back to our tree, but unsurprisingly I can't think of a single one. However, by the time Aikai calls us back to cook our supper I find myself carrying the rear end of the bronze fox up the stairs and into our kitchen.

"Mmm, this is good," Eilsel says happily, after taking a few bites of her meal.

"I'm impressed you could carry a fox this big home!" Aikai says.

"I helped!" I exclaim, although I can see Eilsel smirking from the corner of my eye.

It is almost dark, so I don't think Aikai noticed.

"Can I be excused, please?" I ask after a little while.

"Mmhm," Aikai replies while reading the *Aviaren Times*.

The headline reads: *Fantasticals: Real or Fake??*

I put my plate away and go to my room.

My part of the room has mint green walls. I chose the color when I was six. I've always liked the color green, but now the mint seems too babyish. My room has two walls filled with bookshelves. I've read every book I own at least once. Some of them are mysteries, some are fantasy, but most of them are adventure. There's nothing I love more than adventure. Maybe I like the chilling feeling of getting caught, or the fun of exploring the forest. I think most of all I love adventure because of Eilsel. She's the only friend I have so I might as well have a good time with her.

Eilsel is at one of my bookshelves on my side of our room.

"I'm borrowing some of your books," she announces.

"No you aren't," I reply.

"C'mon, you haven't read most of these since you were like nine."

I sigh. "Fine, you can borrow one book."

Eilsel reluctantly puts five of the books in her arms back on my shelf and takes one to her side of the room. She sits on her bed and begins to read.

When I wake up the next morning the sun is low in the sky. The birds sit on the branches and the squirrels climb our tree. Aikai is at his work bench tinkering with some materials he's found. I can hear his tools clicking against his metal materials.

I open my window and the frost presses against my hands. I put on a sweater and pants. While I get a hat and gloves from my closet, some snow drifts onto my bedroom floor, creating a white blanket.

I step out of my room through the window. Holding onto the branch above my head as I swing my other leg out as well. Beneath me there is a ten-foot drop onto rock and ice. I carefully step from one branch to another until I'm at the base of the tree. Almost every morning I escape through my window. Outside feels like a whole other world waiting to be explored. But sometimes I wonder if there is more to the world, more to life that lingers off in the distance. A life that sometimes I wish I had.

Suddenly, a deer prances by. Its coffee-colored fur and pearl-white dotted markings blur as it disappears into the forest. Spotting little blue dots on a nearby bush, I walk closer to investigate. I realize the bush is a blueberry bush. The shiny round berries leave a luminescent feeling in the air. I pick some for breakfast. I'm probably already late. Once I return home there are only three blueberries left in my pocket.

By mid-morning, Eilsel is already packing for hunting.

"Ready to go?" Eilsel asks me.

"Sure," I say flatly.

Of course I don't want to go hunting. In fact, I hate hunting, but it's not like I have anything better to do.

"Hmmm, did you know Betty Close's egg just hatched?" Aikai asks, although I'm not sure if he's talking to me or to Eilsel.

"Well, I do know that the egg was a spotted one," Eilsel reminds us.

"Really? Spotted? That's one rare egg," I say.

Eilsel grabs her arrow and belt with her bows and heads out the door of our tree house. As we get further from our tree, I hear a loud cry coming from above.

"Eilsel, let's go check on the fledgling," I propose.

The Closes are a beautiful owl family, and even if their new egg wasn't a rare spotted one, I'm sure I wouldn't have been able to stop

18

thinking about them. It's cool to see the Closes all together—I guess since I've never had real parents.

"What fledgling?" she asks, clueless.

"You know which fledgling." I wait for her to respond but when she never does, I remind her, "Betty's egg that just hatched?"

"Oh yeah, I knew that."

I can't help but smile, Eilsel has the goofy look on her face that she gets when she realizes she's forgotten something.

"So what do you say, should we go?" I ask again.

"You bet!"

We walk around a bit until we find the tree with the baby. Ted, Aikai's friend, Betty Close's husband, is there, too. They already have one child (or as Eilsel calls them, Owl-Kids), a boy, but he's always complaining and super annoying.

"Hey, I think I found a good way to spy on them," Eilsel declares.

"Where?"

"Well, we could climb this tree and then sit on that branch while peering through the window." Eilsel points to the different branches while explaining her plan.

I walk up to the tree. It towers over us, casting a shadow from the sun. I put my hands on the tree, holding onto a knot of wood to use as a handle. I have so much practice climbing down our tree from my window that it feels easy to climb almost anything.

Well, it turns out that climbing this tree is not easy.

I'm not even at the first branch when Eilsel yells, "Ready for me to come up?"

I shake my head. "No, it's harder than I thought."

I struggle to lift my foot from one wood knot to the next, then reach up with my hands to grab the one a bit further up. It takes some grunting and pushing until I am finally on the first branch.

"Okay, you can come up now!" I yell down to Eilsel.

She begins to climb. It takes her a little while to get going, but after a few minutes she gets the hang of it.

"I'm almost there!" she shouts.

"I know—I can see you," I reply.

Eilsel takes another step up, her feet pulling upward only because her arms make them. She reaches out for my hand. I reach for hers and finally we are both at the first branch.

The rest of the climb is easy. The final branch leads straight to the Close's window. Inside there's a little white crib that holds a small infant Owl-Aviaren. It's a boy. He already has a nice patch of chestnut feathers. His eyes are hazel. He has claws instead of fingernails and a mask on his face like the other owls. His mother is across the room making a bottle for him. His father is sitting in the chair next to the crib.

"Aww, he's so cute!" Eilsel says.

"Shhhh," I remind her.

Betty is now ready with the bottle. She lifts the baby into her arms and sits in the chair next to Ted.

"Time for your bottle, Sven," Betty sings in a childish voice.

"*Sven*," I repeat to myself.

His mom feeds him the bottle. I can hear Sven's sucking all the way outside the window. After a few minutes, his eyes flutter shut. At that very moment everything feels safe and warm, as if the whole world has paused to take in Betty's sweet song as Sven falls asleep.

SHOOTING THE MOON

EILSEL PAWZORD

We finally returned from spying on the whiny owl-kid. I mean, he was pretty cute once he was asleep, but that only kinda counts. The rest of the time he was still whining. I don't entirely understand why Eoz loves spying on the other Owl-Aviarens. It's honestly a bit stalker-like, but it seems to make her happy. And usually, if Eoz is happy, I'm happy.

Now we get to do my favorite thing: a nighttime hunting trip. Well, it's not my absolute favorite thing to do, but it used to be. Before that stupid Demon-Bear ruined it for me. I've been slightly on edge ever since.

But enough about that, I have to get my hunting stuff. I grab my belt and put it on, then fill the pouches with arrows and my carving knife.

I sling my bow over my back and put on a dark blue cloak with a hood. Then, I put on some hunting trousers.

"Eilsel! Are you ready to go yet?" Eoz shouts.

Eoz can scream *really* loudly. She's all the way down on the forest floor, but I can hear her all the way up in our room, which is one of the higher points of the treehouse.

"Yeah, I'm coming!" I yell in response.

I leap out the window and onto the tree. Then I begin the slow and tedious process of climbing down. It's only in these situations that I envy Aikai's wings. He can just fly up and down. When I reach the balcony, I run inside, down the stairs, and out the door.

I can see that Eoz is wearing a dark green tunic with no hood and some leggings, a stark comparison to the clothes I'm wearing. I'm not the only one to notice this, though.

"Eilsel, come on! Anyone is going to be able to see you out there, what with your bright blue clothing!" Eoz says.

"It's dark blue. It blends in with the night. Plus, it's my favorite color. Additionally, soldiers were here yesterday, and they don't usually come back for months," I state.

Eoz ignores my comment on the soldiers and responds with, "Green is so much more sensible. You can't see my clothes because they're the same color as all the trees and bushes."

I speed up. Aikai is waiting for us up the rundown dirt path, which is lined with pebbles. A stream runs through the clearing, and Eoz and I have spent many days playing there.

"Okay you two, don't run into any Demon-Bears. Got it?" he jokes.

I laugh uneasily and nod. No one knows exactly what I saw back there, just that there was a Demon-Bear and I fell out of a tree. It isn't really something I feel comfortable joking about.

"See you, Aikai!" Eoz waves and we head off.

Aikai hasn't come with us on a hunting trip since we were six. Actually, no, that's not true. After the Demon-Bear incident, he came with us a few times because I was ultra paranoid at that point.

It made me feel like a baby, but I got back into the swing of things eventually. Still, every time the Demon-Bear is brought up, I try to change the topic as quickly as possible. I never want to have to relive that moment again.

I walk forward as slowly as possible, so as not to disturb the animals. I do need to hunt them after all, and I can't do that if they're all running away. Eoz tries to mimic my steps behind me to no avail, but I'm glad that she's trying.

It's funny, because in general, I'm a very clumsy person. However, whenever I'm hunting, it's like I gain supernatural reflexes. I go from being clumsy, immature me to becoming focused, deadly-hunter me. Aikai once likened me to a wolf, slowly stalking my prey.

I hear a crackle behind us and I spin around, almost expecting to see the devilish red eyes of a Demon-Bear. I don't. It's just a sparrow.

"Aren't you going to shoot it?" Eoz asks me.

"Nah. It's not meaty enough to make much food. Besides, look." I point towards a tree illuminated by the moon.

There's a small nest, and tiny birds are sleeping quietly.

"Oh," she says. "I wouldn't want to hurt their mother. You're right, let's keep going."

We trudge forward into the night, getting farther and farther away from the treehouse.

"Eilsel, it's getting late, maybe we should turn back?" Eoz suggests.

"No, wait. Just a little longer and then we'll get to the bear den," I say.

Wait... I meant the area where there are lots of deer, not the bear den! Oh gosh, I can't back down now, or else she'll know just how scared I am to go looking for bears again.

"Eilsel, are you sure? You do remember what happened last time, right?"

"Yeah, I know, but I got this. Trust me!" I say, trying to look confident.

I run in the direction of the bear cave, but eventually I slow down and Eoz catches up to me.

"Eilsel, I've been meaning to ask you this, but what exactly happened with the Demon-Bear? I know it jumped at you and you fell out of a tree or something, and that you were really scared of bears afterwards."

I stop short. I was not expecting that. She's not wrong, though. I was afraid of bears after the Demon-Bear attacked me, but I'm not anymore. The Demon-Bear still scares me, though.

"Listen, I get if it brings back bad memories or if you're scared or—"

"No. I'm not scared," I lie. "I'll tell you what happened. Besides, it's all in the past, right?" I say, trying to assure myself more than her.

"It happened on the day we turned ten, which would be two years ago as of tomorrow. And three years before that, Aikai had promised he'd teach me how to hunt a bear when I turned ten. I still remember when he told me that. 'Aikai, when will I hunt a bear?'" I say, using a cute little voice to mimic younger me.

Eoz laughs. "Go on," she says, smiling.

"So then Aikai replied, "When you're older and wiser.' I didn't know when I would be older and wiser, so I asked him. His answer was, 'How about when you're ten?' I wasn't happy about that either. I wanted to hunt a bear right there and then, but of course you know that I didn't try until our tenth birthday."

Eoz frowned. "That doesn't make any sense. You tried to hunt a bear for the first time when we were eight."

I shake my head and walk a little faster. "No, Aikai stopped me before I got anywhere."

"Oh," Eoz says.

I continue talking. "I'll cut to the chase. The moon was high in the sky, so I could hear wolves howling. I was incredibly excited. I raced out into the night with my bow in my hands. I never put it back on my belt. Aikai said we would be extremely lucky if we found a bear. I knew I had to find one—I wanted to so badly. Of course, I had a reason. Aikai had said he found a bear when he turned eleven, so knew I had to beat him."

"Classic Eilsel," Eoz snorts.

"This is where you come in. You were shivering and everything. I told you it wasn't that cold, and you pretty much growled at me, 'Go away!'"

"I did have a bit of a temper then, didn't I?" Eoz chuckles.

I nod in response.

"Then Aikai suddenly stopped, as if frozen. I'm pretty sure you remember this part."

"Yeah, he was all like, 'We need to go back,'" Eoz tells me.

"Of course I asked him why, because as you know, I really wanted to find that bear. I thought I could find it. I just needed to sneak off when

Aikai wasn't looking... and I did. I should've realized that if Aikai said we needed to go back, it must have been dangerous."

I pause, glaring internally. But not at Eoz. At myself.

"The night went on, and I didn't see a bear for a long, long time. But then I heard a growl. I turned around, and there stood this giant bear. It had black fur with sharp, dangerous red eyes, and teeth that were way too large for my liking."

I shiver. The mere memory is terrifying, and has haunted my nightmares for years. I don't have bad dreams very often, thankfully, but when I do... trust me, it's not fun.

I continue on with the frightening tale.

"I took a step back and drew my bow, which I had kept in my hands literally the whole time. I thought I had the bear. But it jumped forward and attacked, and I barely dodged. Well, then I was stupid and decided to smile at it, of all things. I didn't want it to be easy–"

"Okay, so you're telling me that you *smiled* at the thing that you're currently terrified of?" Eoz asks in an accusatory tone.

I shrug. "Why I ever thought it was a good idea to smile at the bear, I don't know. After I did, I jumped up onto a tree and quickly scrambled to the top. Bears can climb trees, so it followed. Suddenly, I had a stupid, crazy idea. If you were there, you would've definitely told me not to do it. You would have said that I should have climbed down that stupid tree and run as fast as I could away from there. Aikai would probably have said the same."

"Oh no, Eilsel, what stupid thing did you do this time?"

"Come on! Not everything I do is stupid!"

"Hmm... did you decide to swim with the Fins in the stream, or become an Aviaren and fly from the top of our treehouse?" Eoz ponders.

"Hey, that only happened *once!*"

"Just get to the point, Eilsel," my sister says.

"Fine. Well, I jumped toward a branch a little way down. I figured that I could land there, turn around, and stab the Demon-Bear. But in the end, the bear was faster than I was. Before I could twist around and leap at it, the bear raised one giant paw and extended its claws in my direction. The Demon-Bear grinned deviously in a way only a bear could, and I wasn't able to get out of the way of the bear's paw in time."

I stop walking and shudder in a way I hope isn't too visible. I don't want Eoz thinking that I'm as timid as a cowardly Bouldax.

The Bouldax are a race of insect-like humanoids that submitted to the Aurorans' control without hesitation. They're supposedly the best weaponsmiths in all the land, and their home, the Bouldaxian Desert, is said to have the strongest iron in existence.

"Later, I learned that what I saw was a Demon-Bear. Just an illusion—at least Aikai said it was. But anyway, falling from a tree... that wasn't fake. I didn't stop hunting, as you know, because I love it too much, but I knew I needed to be a lot more careful," I conclude.

Eoz looks at me in complete shock. "I... I didn't know it was that bad."

I shrug. "It could've been worse."

"No, it couldn't have! Tell me Eilsel, how scared of the Demon-Bear are you?" Eoz shouts.

"Eoz, it's fine! Sure, maybe it's a little terrifying, but I can deal!" I reply loudly.

Eoz looks behind me in shock. "Eilsel, do you see that? It... it has these glowing red eyes..."

I whip around in panic. Is it here? Has it come back to finish me off? But there's nothing there.

"Eoz! You tricked me!" I say angrily.

"Yes, but it confirmed my theory. You *are* still paranoid!" she yells.

"Listen, what's done is done! It doesn't matter! Just... just forget I ever told you this story! Come on, we have deer to hunt!"

I walk away from Eoz, trying to get away from all the bad memories that our conversation has just brought up.

"Hey, weren't we hunting bears—"

"No! I meant deer!" I shout.

She's right, I'm sure she is. I *am* still scared of the Demon-Bear, and I know it. Now I guess Eoz knows too. But I don't want to have to think about it. I don't want to have to relive it. I don't want to have anything to do with it. But my fear is going to keep coming up. That bear... I sigh.

I turn back to Eoz and apologize for shouting at her. I don't yell very often, but when I do, I know that I need to say sorry.

I'm trying to forget about the incident, but I probably won't ever really. Not when it comes to the Demon-Bear.

WAR CRY

EOZ PAWZORD

At last, it's the morning of my birthday.

I wake up so early that the moon is still out and the stars are still shining. On Eilsel's side of the room I can barely see her sound asleep in bed. I creep down the stairs to see if Aikai is awake. Unfortunately he isn't.

I go upstairs back to our room and take my favorite book off the shelf, *The Knights of Magic*. I turn on my lamp and begin to read. The words are so familiar to me, like a song I memorized by heart. The characters feel so real, like old friends I haven't seen in so long. By the time I finish the chapter, Eilsel rolls out of bed and hits her head on the floor. I ignore her as she rubs her eyes and gets back into bed.

While I lay in bed, I think about the coming day. Of course we would do all the usual things, opening gifts, eating my favorite food and visiting Ted and Betty. Normally, visiting the Closes is boring. We'd go to their treehouse for the afternoon and Aikai would catch up with Ted while Betty made dinner. Eilsel and I would sit around awkwardly for what feels like eternity.

Finally Eilsel wakes up.

"C'mon let's go downstairs!" I whisper excitedly to her.

Aikai is making breakfast. I can tell because of the clattering pots and pans. The room is dark so I draw the drapes. When I open them, I turn back and see Eilsel. Shocked, I scream so loudly that the entire forest must hear me.

"Eilsel, you have wolf ears and—and a tail." I tremble as I speak.

"And you have wings–actual wings," Eilsel replies.

I run downstairs, thoughts racing through my head. "Aikai, Aikai! I have wings! Eilsel has ears! We've been cursed!"

Tears fill my eyes. Eilsel, who is following behind me, murmurs words in a language that may or may not exist.

"Oh my word!" Aikai stammers through a bite of worm toast.

"We've been cursed!" I repeat.

"No, no, you weren't cursed," he pauses and looks up from his scroll. "Come, sit down, and I'll explain."

"You knew about this!" Eilsel shouts.

Aikai doesn't say anything. He looks sorrowful, and shifts nervously in his chair.

Sitting on our old crimson couch I learn what my life really has in store. How dangerous I am. Most importantly, I learn what sacrifices I'll have to make.

"You two aren't actually human," Aikai starts, although he looks apprehensive.

Eilsel and I both nod in unison.

"You are actually Fantasticals."

I gasp. "But, that can't be."

"Fantasticals?" Eilsel asks.

"Yes, you and your sister are both Fantasticals—the only species that can create their own magic."

Eilsel looks astonished. "You're telling me that *we* can create magic?"

Aikai nods. "But in this case, that's not very good."

I know about Fantasticals from books and legends, but they were always the villain or monster, nothing magical or fascinating.

"Are Fantasticals bad?" I ask softly.

Aikai strokes his feathers. "In theory I suppose they can be, but that's also a stereotype. I have known some quite wonderful Fantasticals in my time."

I nod. "But then why do people think Fantasticals are bad?"

"Well, that's a tough question, Eoz. It's hard to tell actually. I suppose a while back, Fantasticals had very little territory even though there were so many of them. They had a great friendship with the Bouldax, though. The Bouldax had plenty of space so they often shared territory with the Fantasticals. In return, the Fantasticals granted the Bouldax magic powers, so that they could be magical as well. However, one day the chief Fantastical fell very ill and not long after that he passed on. They say he returned to the essence of magic. But when he left this world, the ability to share magic disappeared along with him. The Fantasticals could no longer give anyone power, so the Bouldax grew very angry. So angry, in fact, that the Bouldax kicked the Fantasticals out of their territory. They started telling the other factions that the Fantasticals were terrible creatures, even though they'd done nothing wrong at all. Eventually, the Bouldax declared war on the Fantasticals. Unfortunately, the rest of the seven factions joined them."

"So, were Fantasticals killed off?" I ask.

"Not exactly. Some survived, but not many. They live in small forests across the world, like this one. When the two of you were born, you had one Fantastical parent and one human parent. Your mom, a Fantastical unicorn, hid her unicorn traits from your dad for many years. When you were born she had no choice but to tell your dad. When he found out, he was furious. He was so mad that he told the Auroran general in his area. Over the past twelve years, they have been creating an army to defeat you and all of the Fantasticals that still remain," Aikai finishes.

There is a moment of dead silence.

Finally, Eilsel asks, "So, how did she hide our animal traits?"

Aikai starts playing with his feathers, something he does only when he's nervous. "Your mother was a very smart woman, the smartest I knew. That night when your father ran away, only the day after you were born, your mom casted an extremely strong spell on the two of you. She made it so your animal traits wouldn't show for twelve years. She thought that would be long enough. Unfortunately, only a couple days later, a small army was sent out to kill her. They succeeded."

All color drains from Eilsel's face. I gasp. I still have a million questions, but right now I can only think of my mother's atrocious death.

Aikai looks away. We can tell that he was very close to my mother, so talking about her death must've been really hard for him.

After a moment he continues, "I think it's still important to celebrate with the Closes. It would be quite rude to cancel at the last minute."

Eilsel and I both nod.

"We will leave their house right after dusk so we have enough time to train your Fantastical traits. We don't want it to be too dark, but I'm sure Eilsel won't have a problem with that."

I look at my twin uneasily.

She knits her eyebrows as if to reply, "I don't know what he's talking about either."

Aikai seems to have a way of reading our thoughts. "Ahh, you are probably wondering what kind of Fantasticals you are. Eilsel, you are a sort of Shadow Wolf Fantastical, or that's what I think, but I'm not completely sure. That's why you have night vision. You also have enhanced hearing. Eoz, you are a Griffin Fantastical. Tonight I'll teach you to fly, and you'll be able to hunt much more easily with your brand new talons. Also, tonight make sure you cover all of your physical traits. No one can know you are Fantasticals."

I look at Eilsel, she looks at me. We had never even heard of griffins or weird types of wolves. How did he expect us to know how to use our Fantastical traits?

I look through my closet. What could possibly cover two giant white wings? Most of my sweaters are too thin. And a blouse won't cover anything. I decide on my red cloak. It's just long enough to cover the tips of my wings. Everything else is simple. I will wear a hat for my ears and gloves for my talons. I put everything on and to my surprise, I look just like a normal girl in the snow.

"C'mon, we're leaving, Eoz!" Eilsel shouts from down stairs.

"Coming!" I reply.

Eilsel is also wearing gloves and a hat to cover her ears and claws. Her long bushy tail is tucked into the side of her pants.

Once we start walking, I ask, "Does anyone know we are Fantasticals?"

"All of Aurora does. They know there are two Fantastical girls somewhere around here."

"Thanks to our father," Eilsel murmurs.

About halfway to the Close's tree, for the first time I notice a crumpled piece of paper pasted to a tree. The letters are smudged, but I can barely make out the words FANTASTICAL WANTED. I can't believe my eyes. How could I have never seen these posters before?

Ding dong, the doorbell rings.

"Hello girls! Nice to see you. Come in!" Betty says cheerfully as she answers the door.

Ted is rocking the baby.

"Let me take your coats," Betty offers.

"Umm, no thank you," I say politely.

She gives me a funny look but doesn't say anything. We all sit in the living room.

"We haven't seen you all in so long. How are things?" Ted asks.

"Pretty good," Aikai answers before we can even open our mouths.

The adults continue to talk until the little beep goes off from the oven and it's time for dinner.

"The vegetable pie is delicious!" Eilsel says with her mouth full.

"Manners," Aikai reminds her.

Sven sits in a little grey chair between Betty and me. He has a bowl of mashed carrots and peas that Betty feeds him one tiny bite at a time.

"Is everyone ready for dessert?"

We all cheer in response.

Everyone sings Happy Birthday, then we cut the chocolate birthday cake. Ted hands out the cake to everyone including Sven, who smashes it more than he eats it. After dessert, we all return to the couch.

Eilsel and I wait patiently for the clock to strike 9:45. Even Aikai looks anxious. He normally enjoys the hours he spends with Ted, but today he is focusing more on what is yet to come tonight.

"Eilsel, Eoz! I almost forgot your birthday presents," Ted hands us the two packages while grinning from ear to ear.

I unwrap mine first. Inside there is a beautiful necklace with a gold chain and a teal crystal.

"I picked it out for you—the crystal is called a Grandidierite," Betty informs me.

"Thank you so much. I love it!"

Betty puts the necklace on my neck while Eilsel opens her gift. I'm not joking. Eilsel's face turns bright red.

"By the nine factions, this is the best gift ever!" Eilsel screams with delight.

Her package contains a deep redwood colored leather journal. Her full name, 'Elisel Pawzord,' is engraved on the front.

Aikai smiles. "I don't think I can beat that!" he says as he takes two small presents out of his pocket. "Here."

Each package holds a beautiful bronze watch. I put mine on and wind it to the right time. The watch's hands tic as though pushed by the wind, smooth and graceful.

"Thank you, Aikai!" I say.

"Yes, thank you! They are awesome!" Eilsel adds.

Aikai continues to speak with the Close's, until my watch finally reads 9:45. We say our goodbyes, and leave the Close's tree.

FLYING FREE

EOZ PAWZORD

"Where are we going now?" Eilsel asks.

"Shhh," I chirp.

At first we get close to our tree, but we end up walking away from it when we turn towards the creek. There's a little hill on the west side of the creek, and at the top, a series of rocks pile up to create a sort of cliff.

Sometimes Eilsel and I jump off the rocks into the creek. If it's not too cold, that is. When we were younger we would spend hours jumping off the rock. Occasionally there would be a young Aviaren child with their mother or father, but we knew this place better than anyone.

When we get to the top, I see a few Fins swimming downstream.

"Take off your jackets," Aikai instructs.

Even though it is freezing cold, I obey Aikai and do so anyway.

"Oh, and your hat and gloves," he adds.

We put our clothing in a pile on the rocks. I look at Eilsel and take a real good look at her tail.

"We really look like animals," I mutter under my breath.

I'm not sure if I'm liking this, but it's our mothers faction. We have to embody it, right? And besides, having wings could be great. I remember when I was younger I was so curious about Aikai's wings. I had always longed for wings of my own. I guess my dream has finally come true.

"Eilsel, your training will be first," Aikai announces.

"Okay," she replies.

"You will first learn how to use your enhanced hearing."

She nods.

"Eoz and I will go across the creek and have a conversation. You are going to try your best to eavesdrop from over here," He explains.

Eilsel nods again. "Okay."

Aikai and I get off the cliff and cross the river. The water is colder than usual so I try my best to run through the ankle deep water as fast as I can.

When we get to the other side, Aikai says, "Okay Eoz, all you have to do is talk to me. We're are going to see how strong Eilsel's hearing is."

I flash him a thumbs up. Well, I suppose now it's more of a talons up.

"Eoz, did you know that there is a Demon-Bear around here somewhere?" Aikai asks me in a low voice.

"Really? Should we try to hunt it?" I reply, knowing he is only saying that to test my twin's hearing rather than suggesting that we actually hunt one.

"I don't know, it could be dangerous. Maybe Eilsel should come with us," Aikai says.

I smile. "If you say so."

After we finish talking, Aikai flies up to the miniature cliff that Eilsel is standing on.

"How much of that could you hear?" he asks.

"All of it. it sounded like you were right next to me," Eilsel replies.

Aikai waves back over to me and gives me an okay sign. He then signals for me to come back to the cliff.

I slosh back through the water and the bottom of my pants start to get wet. The tips of my wings dip through the water as well.

"Nice job, Eilsel. I think that's enough training for now. Eoz, It's time I teach you how to fly," Aikai says calmly like flight is something he does every day. I mean I guess he does, he is an owl after all. "First, try to flap your wings."

"Okay, I'll try."

I try to flap my wings but it's hard at first. Almost like when your arm or leg falls asleep. I'm not used to having extra limbs attached to my body. After a couple tries I flap my wings at a steady pace.

"Good, now try jumping a little bit," Aikai says.

I jump a few inches into the air. It feels as if nothing's happening, but when I reach the ground I land slower and more precisely. As I jump a bit higher, I can feel myself floating in the air and then drifting down like a leaf.

"Very nice, now let's see if you can really fly!" Aikai exclaims.

"No, I'm not jumping off!" I squeal.

Sure, I've jumped off this rock before, but not in the dark and certainly not with wings.

"Oh, relax! If you do it right then you'll fly right up in the air. It's easy!"

"Yeah, but what if I do it wrong! I could fall into the stream!"

"So what? The current's not strong at all. Just get back up and swim to the bank. Besides, stop worrying about what could go wrong. Focus on what could go right."

I hesitate, but I will myself to put my feet on the edge. The ground below me seems loose and unstable. It feels as if I'll take one step and the whole world will crumble. I take a breath and count to three in my head. Then, I jump.

I leap out into the night. At first, I feel myself falling. I'm sure I'll crash and tumble into the stream. But then I realize that I'm not falling anymore. I'm actually hovering about five feet over the water. I use what Aikai had taught me and pump my wings back and forth. Eventually, I fly above where Aikai and Eilsel are standing.

"You got this!" I hear Eilsel shout from below.

"You can stop flapping now!" Aikai explains.

I stop my wings. I don't fall, I don't crash, but I soar. I fly down and dip my wing into the water. I flap my wings upward and fly to the treetops. I finally feel free.

Yet I can't understand how something so beautiful like Fantasticals could be evil.

Or are they?

The night air feels cold against my skin as the wind blows through my wings. A dark shadow flies through the sky off in the distance. It doesn't look like a bird, but more like a humanoid. Why would someone be out this late? Are they looking for someone?

I decide to not think much about it, and instead go back down to the rock where Aikai and Eilsel are waiting for me.

"Great job!" Eilsel shouts.

"Thanks!" I chime.

"All right, that's enough flying for one day," Aikai announces.

Eilsel smiles wearing a proud expression on her face. Aikai leads us to some trees near the stream. When we were little he told us that these trees were the reason why this forest is called the *Peril* Forest. After that day I've never found the courage to enter those trees.

When Aikai leads us toward the trees, he doesn't warn us about anything dangerous or scary. Instead he tells us that our mother used to live here.

SON OF FIRE

EILSEL PAWZORD

I can't believe it. Me, Eoz... Fantasticals? I just don't understand. In all the stories, Fantasticals are evil beings who destroy towns and break promises. So how could we be them? I've never destroyed *anything*, much less a town. (I mean, unless you count rooms.) Aikai says Fantasticals are good and insists that the stories are wrong, but he might just be trying to comfort us.

I sigh. I don't want to think about this. It's too early. Too early for me to be awake, much less for me to be getting dressed. But that's what happens when a random human dumb enough to come into our forest sees Eoz flying in the sky with bird wings. Correction, I mean Griffin wings.

Anyway, Aikai was flying through the sky last night, doing his normal owl thing, when he saw someone running to the town a few miles from our forest. How someone could run that fast, I don't know, but Aikai followed them.

The human eventually reached an Auroran military base near a village and started to talk to the commanding officer there. Aikai had swooped low to hear what they were discussing. Turns out, the human had seen us. The human knew who we were, and this was not good.

Aikai immediately turned to fly back to us, but one of the archers saw him and shot at him, thinking he was Eoz. Somehow, he still managed to get back to our treehouse, even with an arrow in his wing. He told us that we needed to go, that we needed to leave and find somewhere safe to hide.

And that is why I'm currently getting dressed at approximately three o'clock in the morning. I pack a bag with essentials: food, water, hunting equipment. Eoz says I'm stupid to bring hunting stuff (it's too heavy!) but her bag is laden down with books, so she isn't one to talk.

I climb down to the kitchen floor. Aikai and Eoz are already there.

"Slow poke," Eoz mutters.

"Now is not the time for arguing. As I said earlier, you need to go." Aikai nurses his injured wing. "And I cannot come with you."

I look at Eoz in shock, and then back to Aikai. "No! You have to come!"

"If you stay, the soldiers will find you," Eoz murmurs worriedly.

"No, they won't. We Owl-Aviarens have places we can hide if we need to, but you would not be able to come." Aikai pauses, as if reconsidering and looks at Eoz. "No, actually, that isn't right. It is possible that *you* could come."

I panic for a moment. Would Aikai and Eoz really leave me behind?

"But then again," Aikai continues. "Eoz probably couldn't make the flight yet. And I wouldn't leave you behind, Eilsel... so the best bet for both of you best is to hide in a town called Starlight."

Aikai pulls out a map and gestures to a spot a little away from the forest marked 'Starlight'.

"Hide here for a bit, and eventually I will come find you. Eoz, practice your flying. Eilsel, try not to gain any weight, okay?" Aikai jokes.

I assume he means he would have to carry me to the Owl-Aviaren's hiding place. "Well, you never know, maybe I'll sprout wings too."

Eoz keeps a straight face.

"Do you have everything?" Aikai asks.

We nod.

"In that case," he says. "I love you both. Stay safe, and don't get into trouble. I need to go warn the other owls the moment the sun rises."

Aikai hugs us, and we exit the treehouse—our home—for what might be the final time.

"Wait!" Aikai exclaims, flapping his wings in a type of run-glide to catch up to us.

"Remember the watches I gave you for your birthdays? Wear them. They should be able to hide your Fantastical features. I used magic gifted to me in the form of a crystal to infuse them with power. They shouldn't run down for a while, so don't worry."

Aikai hugs us again. I can tell letting us go is hard for him too. But we still have to leave. Nothing can change that.

I try not to look back at the treehouse as we run into the distance, but it's nearly impossible. Tears fill my eyes, but I will not cry. *I'm brave*, I think to myself. We started this whole mess, so we must be able to also get ourselves out of it, right?

For the next ten minutes, neither Eoz nor I speak.

Finally, Eoz breaks the silence. "Eilsel, I've been thinking. Aikai isn't all that strong. He tries to pretend he is, but we all know he isn't. His wing didn't look like it would get any better," Eoz pauses and closes her eyes. "Do you think that he'll survive?"

She has said what neither of us wanted to put into words. I swallow hard and then say, "Probably not."

The sun begins to rise up over the trees.

"Right now we need to focus."

"Uh-huh."

I can tell she doesn't want to talk, so I just keep moving. After a bit, we start to hear noise. It sounds like... marching, maybe?

"Stop," Eoz commands.

The noises get closer, and we hide in a bush, afraid of what we know we're going to see.

"Troops," I whisper.

My sister nods. At the head of the battalion is a young man. No wait, he's younger than that. Maybe a teenager? Fourteen, fifteenish?

"Sir, if we keep going at this pace, the men won't be able to fight once we get there," an advisor says timidly.

"I've told you, Advisor, we need to keep moving."

"Sir, we really need to rest," a boy even younger than the commander croaks.

The commander's face softens. "Very well, Red."

The rest of the battalion sighs in relief. They start to set up camp, and the commander and 'Red' sit nearest our bush.

"Thanks for letting us rest, Agni!"

"I've told you, Brother, while we're in public it's *sir*,"

"Riiiiight, Big Bro." Red grins.

"Soldier Red, I get that you're only twelve, but you have to be more serious. We are on a march to capture two very dangerous people."

"But why are they dangerous? You said they're twelve, just like me. How can two kids be such a big—what's that word you used the other day? Oh yeah, threat. How are they such a big threat?"

I almost laugh out loud. This kid's pretty funny.

"One is a confirmed Griffin Fantastical, and we can assume the other is a Fantastical as well, but of what kind we do not know. Fantasticals are horrible monsters, remember? That's why we need to wipe them all out."

Commander Agni glares at Red, annoyed as though he's said these words at least a hundred times before.

"Yeah, I know." Red fidgets for a moment before continuing. "Just like the prophecy says! Hawken's gonna kill the monsters and save us all!"

Excellent. That's exactly what we need. *More* people trying to kill us.

Agni looks absolutely livid for a moment before returning to his icy stature to say, "Right."

Red looks around to see if anyone is watching, and it looks like no one is. (Joke's on him, we're watching.)

Then he lowers his voice so that I can barely hear. "Why do we have to wear this blue uniform? I liked our old one better."

"You know why," Agni mutters. "Now come on, we have to get back to hunting the monsters so that Hawken can save the world."

I swear there's sarcasm in his voice.

Red sighs. "Yes, sir."

And with that, they're back on the hunt, looking for us. Once they leave, Eoz and I hop out of our hiding spot.

"You know... that kid, Red, would have made a good friend if he wasn't on the side actively trying to capture and kill us," I say.

Eoz groans. "You're so immature, Eilsel."

THE BIRD AND THE SCYTHE

EOZ PAWZORD

The trees come to an end and the city begins. There are little kids running around and parents trying to catch them. As we get closer to the city, I can see lights draped on all the buildings and trees. Lanterns hang on posts, their yellow light shining like miniature suns.

"Is that the Starlight Festival?"

We have never been to one, but we know they exist from books we've read.

"Yeah, look at that sign!" Eilsel points to a banner high above our heads.

It reads, *Starlight Festival! Open from sunset today 'til sunset tomorrow.* It isn't quite sunset yet, but most booths are starting to open. I haven't noticed how hungry I am until I smell the various food stands all across the festival grounds.

"C'mon, let's go get some food," I say.

I have ten coins in my pocket and Eilsel also has ten.

"Okay, sure," she replies.

As we walk through the festival, we see people wearing costumes and masks. Some adults are getting ready for the parade, and many children are playing with ribbons and other sewing materials. Every food stand we pass has a long line, even the ones that haven't opened yet. The one that has the shortest line is the tart stand, so we decide to follow in line.

Over by the tart stand, there are two kids sitting on a rock, one boy and one girl. The girl has almond-colored hair and green eyes. The boy has almost red hair and blue eyes. They are both wearing pants and an old shirt. They look tired, like they haven't slept for days.

"Hi, how can I help you?" The lady running the tart stand asks when we make it to the front of the line.

"Can I have a strawberry tart?" Eilsel asks.

"And can I have a banana tart please?" I ask.

"Of course," she replies.

We stand to the side while they make our food.

"Number eighty-six!" Someone calls our number a few minutes later.

"That's us!" Eilsel says as she runs over to retrieve our food.

She hands me my tart and we stand there taking the first bite of food we have had for what feels like a long time.

We both gobble down our food while we walk to some empty picnic tables nearby.

"Umm, hi. I'm so sorry to ask you this, but can we have a coin or two?" I hear someone ask from behind me.

I turn around fast, my hair hitting my face.

"Oh, um hi," I say hesitantly.

Eilsel catches on before I do.

"Yeah, of course." She says as she hands the boy a few Auran gold coins, the national currency of Aurora.

"Thank you!" the boy and the girl standing next to him say happily.

Eilsel and I sit on the rock as we eat our tarts.

Only about a minute has passed when I see the same two kids emerging from the crowd. They are holding a basket of doughnut-holes with chocolate melted on top. They sit down next to us.

"I'm sorry, we haven't properly introduced ourselves," the girl says.

"I'm Eilsel."

"Hi, I'm Eoz."

"Cool, I'm Sciprus. Sciprus Puffin," the boy, who we now know as Sciprus, introduces himself.

"And I'm Wren," the girl announces.

I smile. This is the first time I have ever met a human child and I kind of like it.

"Are you new here? I don't recognize you," Wren exclaims.

"Yeah, we umm, just moved here," I lie.

I know we aren't allowed to tell anyone about us being Fantasticals or living in the Peril forest, so I guess my lie is justified.

They nod, and then both stuff a donut hole into their mouths.

"The Starlight Festival is my favorite day of the year." Sciprus pauses, and then adds more softly, "Well, it used to be my favorite holiday."

"What do you mean?" Eilsel inquires.

"I ran away from home not that long ago. This used to be the one time a year when my family didn't fight."

"Oh," I mutter.

"I'm a runaway too. Sciprus and I were always friends even before we left home. Both of our families acted like we didn't exist. They never cared for us. So one day we decided to run away together," Wren explains.

I sigh, suddenly feeling very touched and a bit sad.

"I'm an orphan too," I mutter so quietly I don't think anyone hears—I suppose Eilsel does. "Yeah, our parents both died when we were a few days old."

I don't want to bring up Aikai at the moment. At this point we don't know where he is or even whether or not he's alive.

Everyone looks down, shaking their heads.

"I'm sorry," Sciprus whispers.

Eilsel is looking at Wren all funny. "Hey, is your name Wren like the bird?"

Wren looks up. "Yeah, my mom liked the bird."

After a long silence, I say quietly, "I wish I had a mom."

"What did you say?" Wren asks.

"Oh, uhh, I said I wish I had a mom." I turn away to hide my face.

Eilsel looks at me, and I see tears forming in the corners of her eyes.

"You don't need a mother, you've got us now," Wren comforts us.

"Yeah, I guess we do."

"Hey, let's go on the horse carriage!" Sciprus decides.

"Okay, but what's a carriage?" I ask.

Wren and Sciprus just start laughing.

Eilsel and I look at them quite strangely.

"A carriage is like a small room on wheels. It's pulled by a horse," Sciprus explains. "Sorry, that's not the most amazing description," he adds as an afterthought.

I nod, but I still can't understand what he meant.

"Well, let's go already!"

"Tickets, tickets come get your tickets! Only 25 cents a piece!" a cheery man calls out.

He wears a red, yellow, and orange top hat and a matching pair of pants and shirt. Wren leads us over to him.

"Would you like some tickets?" the man asks.

"Yes, please," Sciprus replies.

Eilsel gives him two silver coins. We get four tickets in exchange. A long line of people are standing in front of what has to be the waiting zone for the carriage. We wait in line for a very, very long time.

"Next!" a man hollers.

"Finally!" Wren exclaims giddily.

I smile as we hand our tickets to him and board the bright blue carriage.

The horse starts running, and soon the trees are passing by much faster than we could ever run. It feels almost as good as flying.

"Hey look, there's an owl!" Eilsel announces.

"Yeah!" we all agree.

Eilsel's gaze meets mine. We both know why she mentioned the owl—because of Aikai. Even though neither of us has said anything more about it, we are both scared for what's going to happen to him. Would we even find out?

We've gone halfway around the forest when the carriage stops moving.

"Umm, guys, why did it stop?" Sciprus wonders.

I lean over the edge to see if the driver is doing anything to get us moving again. Unfortunately it doesn't look like he is.

"Ehh, we'll be fine. We've survived much worse before," Eilsel says.

"Yeah, don't worry about it. I'm sure it's normal," Wren replies.

Sciprus nods in agreement.

"Let's play a game to pass the time," Wren suggests.

"Okay, what game?" Eilsel asks.

"Hmmm, how about truth or dare?" Wren says.

"Yeah, sure I'll go first." Sciprus agrees.

"Okay, Wren, truth or dare?" Sciprus asks.

"Dare."

I watch Sciprus think of a dare, his eyebrows knit and his hand below his chin. "I dare you to imitate Eoz."

Wren shakes her head. "I barely even know her!"

"That's why it's fun," Sciprus explains.

So Wren stands up and pulls her hair up like I do. Then she smiles shyly. "I'm Eoz, and, um, I'm really smart."

I shake my head, laughing hysterically. "I don't sound like that at all!"

"Well, I tried," Wren says. "All right, my turn! Eilsel, truth or dare?"

Eilsel takes a little while to reply, but eventually she says, "Dare."

"Okay! I have a great one! I dare you to jump up and down really hard to shake the carriage."

"Okay, I'll try," Eilsel says.

She stomps really hard while holding onto one of the walls. The cabin jolts us around moving from side to side.

"Ahhh!" We scream.

To my understanding, this is a lot shakier than the actual ride.

"Okay, okay, make it stop!" Sciprus groans.

Eilsel grabs on to one of the poles and holds it until it the carraige is steady.

"Woah, how'd you do that?" Sciprus asks.

Eilsel shrugs, "I don't know. Truth or dare, Sciprus?"

"Truth," he replies.

Eilsel hesitates for a second but then asks, "Do you ever miss your family?"

Sciprus's cheeks become red and his hands get sweaty.

"Yeah. I do," he finally says.

"Sciprus, do me!" I say, cheerfully.

"Okay, truth or dare?"

I think about it for a minute, before deciding. "Truth."

"What's your deepest, darkest secret?" he inquires.

I realize quickly that I can't really share my secret. "I dunno."

Wren makes a face. "Ohhhh, come on, I know you have secrets. The way you look at us. The way you are so cautious. Out of everyone here you have the most knowledge, the most secrets."

"You know what? Fine," I say, irritated. "I'm a Fantastical."

THE UNICORN

EILSEL PAWZORD

"Wait what?" Sciprus looks at Eoz with eyes wide as the moon.

"What do you mean, you're a Fantastical? T-that's impossible."

"I thought they were extinct," Wren adds.

I look at Eoz. She looks at me.

"Eoz, why'd you say that?" I ask. "Aikai specifically said, 'Don't tell anyone' or whatever."

Wren stares at me. "That confirms it, then. You're both Fantasticals, aren't you?"

I try not to look guilty. It's too bad, because I'm pretty sure I'm failing at it. Once, on a rainy day when I couldn't go hunting, we played a game of Old Prowl. Basically there's one Prowl card in the game, and the rest are Aurorans. You make matches with the Aurorans, but there's no other Prowl card. If you have the Prowl card at the end of the game, you lose.

So anyway, I drew the Prowl card, and Eoz was supposed to trade cards with me. She only had to take one. I didn't want her to know that I had the card, so I tried doing something Aikai called an Ice-face.

That basically meant that I tried to hide that I was guilty, but it was so obvious I had the Prowl card that Eoz freaked out, saying, "Eilsel has it, I know it!"

I lost that game, and if I ever were to mention it around Eoz, she would laugh in my face.

Wren and Sciprus deduce that they're correct in regards to the whole Fantastical thing.

"We should turn you in," Wren flat-out states.

"Uhh, please don't do that?" I ask as politely as I can.

Wren chuckles. "Of course I won't! I'm just fooling with you. I've never had a Fantastical friend before, much less two!"

I breathe a sigh of relief.

"No one heard that, right?" Sciprus asks cautiously.

"I don't think so," Eoz says. "But we should leave the festival the moment we get off this carraige."

I nod in agreement. The last thing we want is some kid going, "Mommy, what's a Fantastical?"

Thankfully, the carriage starts moving again.

"Sorry about that," the driver apologizes. "The horse was spooked... she must've smelled something funny."

"It's fine, sir," Sciprus affirms.

"I'm sorry, what was that?" the driver asks. "I can't hear very well."

"I said that it's fine, sir," Sciprus says loudly.

The driver looks thankfully at us. "Again, my apologies."

The driver returns to his post, and the horse starts trotting again. We enter a forest that isn't familiar. The trees cast long shadows over one another, and I swear I hear an owl hooting in the distance.

It reminds me a bit of Aikai. He used to hoot whenever he was really happy, which wasn't often right before we left the forest.

"So... anyone know any good stories?" I ask, trying to break the silence.

"You know all mine," Eoz answers.

"We know some. Right, Wren?" Sciprus says.

The girl who has become one of our first human friends nods tentatively, which is kind of weird for her as far as I can tell. She seems talkative and friendly, not shy like Eoz sometimes is.

"Well, there's this crazy story we heard a while back. It seems relevant now, so do you want to hear it?" Scirpus questions.

"Yes, yes, yes again!" I squeal.

Eoz rolls her eyes. Sciprus raises an eyebrow.

"Don't mind her," my twin apologizes. "She's not always like that. Just when it comes to stories."

Wren shrugs. "It's all good. So Sciprus, why don't you start?"

"Right. Once, long, long ago, on the full moon, there was a unicorn. She was brave and smart, and she lived in a forest with magical spirits." Sciprus says 'magical' with a really weird voice. "And then—"

He's interrupted by Wren, "Let's face it, you've officially proven yourself to be a horrible storyteller. I will continue it from here."

Sciprus pouts—pouts!?—for a moment, but doesn't argue.

"So anyway, the unicorn met someone she really loved, but he was a human. A human would never fall in love with a unicorn, she thought, so she disguised herself as a beautiful young woman. It was love at first sight, and soon they were married happily. A time later, the unicorn had twins. But when they were born, the father gasped. The children looked really funny. The father was a good person, but he had a bad habit of condemning anything he deemed ugly (like most of his people), and his children unfortunately fell into that category. He thought the ugliness stemmed from the mother (even though she was quite pretty). The woman was soon revealed as a unicorn, and the father left her and ran off to tell the officials, who he knew would kill his wife and kids. Maybe he would regret this later, but we will never know. The unicorn entrusted her children to one of the magical spirits who owed her a debt (and may or may not have really liked her at one point), and then she ran off into the night. She was killed the next morning. The two children were left to grow up in secret with the magical spirits, and they were never seen again," Wren finished.

"I think I've heard that story before," Eoz says quizzically.

"Me too," I add.

"Wait... Aikai!" Eoz and I shout at the same time.

It's a good thing the horse driver doesn't have very good hearing, because he doesn't turn his head toward us.

Sciprus goes quiet for a moment, then whispers something to Wren. Her eyes go wide, and she nods.

"It's you two, isn't it?" Sciprus asks.

"Uhh, what do you mean by that? I'm confused," I say.

"Well, I mean, maybe, errr, this is weird... but are you, umm..." he stutters.

I honestly don't know what he means. From the look I'm getting from Eoz, she doesn't understand either.

Wren decides to sum it up for us. "You're the ones in the story."

"I never really thought about it before, but you're right. We've definitely heard the story before, and it does sound really similar to ours," Eoz replies, as though this isn't a jaw-dropping discovery.

I'd kind of like to nudge Eoz and tell her to stop spilling all of our secrets, but it's too late now.

I can't really compute. We've heard this story before, several times, actually, and yet I never made the connection between the story and us. Aikai had told this story almost like it was a fairy tale, and also slightly differently. He always told us that the father didn't like the kids because he found out they were Fantasticals. But in Sciprus and Wren's version of the story, we were ugly? Okay, not cool.

"I didn't realize that we were that ugly," I say in mock disdain.

Everyone ignores me, but I now understand that our father called the officials on us and our mom because we're Fantasticals. Before now, I haven't thought of our parents much. It's never been as much of an issue to me, whereas for Eoz, it's basically the opposite. I guess I always thought that it would be cool to meet our parents, but I never asked Aikai where they were. I suppose I just always assumed that they were... gone.

Anyway, I'm half right. But now that I know all this, I also realize our mother must have been amazing. Still, you can't really think of someone as your mom if you didn't really meet them, right? I know Aikai isn't my real father, but he may as well be. And now that I know that my actual dad is a real jerk, I'm glad I've never known him. I'm positive that Aikai is a much better father than our real dad could ever be.

"This is all so confusing," I say, holding my head in my hands. "What are we going to do?"

This time, they don't ignore me.

Wren sighs. "Okay, relax. You need somewhere to hide, and the best place to do that is Star Village Academy."

I look at the two quizzically. "Why?"

Sciprus and Wren look at each other, and I'm sure that their eyes convey a million words. There's something that they're not telling us, but I won't stick my head into things they don't want me to know about. At least, not right now.

"Oh, I just have a feeling. Besides, our parents haven't found us here yet, even though they're probably looking," Wren says, and I have to strain to hear the last part, as her speech trails off into a whisper.

I look at Eoz, who nods. Sciprus seems to agree with Wren, although he doesn't talk nearly as much as her.

"We'll do it," Eoz says, I suppose speaking for the two of us.

Depending on your point of view, this decision could be considered a disaster or a major accomplishment.

HUNTER
AND PREY

EILSEL PAWZORD

I walk up to the school building. It's made of spruce wood in the form of logs, and it actually looks really cool. I'm excited to learn with all those other kids. I've never done that sort of thing before. I was homeschooled by an owl, after all.

We walk into the building, out of the freezing weather. If the Starlight Festival just happened, then it's the beginning of Auran, the season of cold and ice. Next it will be Floran, the season of regrowth and beauty. Then Flaran, the season of heat and fire. Finally, it will be Aguan, the season of preparation and water.

"Who's this, Sciprus?" a lady sitting behind a desk asks kindly.

"Of course you know Wren, who also attends school here, but these two are my cousins. They lived in a forest far away, so school is all new to them. But I can assure you they're very smart and learn things fast," Sciprus answers.

"What are your names, dearies?" the kind woman asks us.

"I'm Eoz, and this is my twin Eilsel. We are honored to be here," my sister answers politely.

"Please could they go to school here for a little, Madam Roselle?" Sciprus pleads.

"Well, they can attend for a week or two, I suppose. Only because it's you, Sciprus." Madam Roselle smiles. "Now in you go, you're going to be late!"

The four of us hurry toward the door that Wren says leads to the main school building, Sciprus shouting one last 'Thank you!' as we go.

I push open the door, and Wren soon takes the lead.

"Okay, follow me! We're in the sixth level of schooling, so we're right over here!" she shouts.

Soon we arrive at a door marked with a '6'. Wren opens the door and takes a seat as fast as possible. Eoz sits right next to her, and Scirpus sits in the front row. There aren't any more chairs available near my friends, so I head to the back row.

A blond haired woman walks through the entrance. I can only assume she's the teacher.

"Good morning Madam Lavourne!" the class choruses.

"And good morning to you too, students. Now I've heard from Madam Roselle that we have two new students. Would you please stand up and introduce yourselves?" Madam Lavourne asks and Eoz stands.

"Hello, I'm Eoz Pawzord. I'm from a forest rather far from here, and I have a twin sister." With that, Eoz sits down.

I fidget with my watch, hoping its power is holding up, and then stand up. "Hello, I'm Eilsel Pawzord. Eoz is my twin, and I like to hunt," I say nervously, sitting down the moment I finish.

Normally I'm good with people... but then there's the fact that almost all the people I know are owls. Madam Lavourne starts talking about a test we'll have in a week about trees and animals of the forest. I smile internally. I could ace that.

"We have PE next, students. You will meet Sir Sprucewood at the grounds in about ten minutes. Meanwhile, you may talk with your peers," Madam Lavourne finishes.

I pull out the journal I got for my birthday. I don't feel like talking.

"Hah, is that your diary?" a boy sitting next to me crows.

Some of his friends laugh.

"One, it's a journal. And two, I haven't written anything in it," I retort in annoyance.

The kid ignores my answer and continues, "Anyway, you said you liked to hunt, right? Bet you I can do it better than you."

I look up and ask, "What's your name?"

"Jeremy," the boy responds. "And you better remember it."

"I'm sure I will, especially if I write it down," I say, and then grin as I write 'Jeremy = Jerk' in my journal.

I flash it in his direction.

"Hey!" Jeremy whisper-yells.

"You said you wanted me to remember it," I remind him.

"He's going to crush you in PE. You'll see," one of his thugs insists.

I give him a wayward smile that says, 'Yeah, sure.' Jeremy glares, and his followers mimic him.

When we arrive at the fields, Sir Sprucewood isn't there yet.

"Sorry I'm late!" a booming voice echoes through the room after a few minutes. "To all you new students, I'm Sir Sprucewood, but you can call me... uh, Sprucewood!"

The students and I follow him through the halls. The PE teacher waves at every student he walks past, and they all wave back or say 'Hey, Sprucewood!' It seems as though he knows every kid in the school. Eventually, we step out into the cold outside.

Many of the students stop there, and look surprised when Sir Sprucewood yells, "Today we're going for the real forest experience!"

The students look at one another fearfully.

"There could be wolves in the forest!" one kid whispers to another.

I roll my eyes. There are always wolves in Peril Forest. I can see Eoz has a similar response to mine.

"Scared, Pawzord? If there are wolves, I bet they'll eat you first!" Jeremy says snidely.

"You wish, Jeremy," I snap back.

Sir Sprucewood walks towards us to ask, "Is there something wrong?"

Jeremy's face changes instantly. "T-this meanie says that wolves are going to eat me!"

Sprucewood turns to me. "Is this true?"

"No! Why would I say that?" I say, appalled.

This boy's one of those kids who is a jerk around other students but a perfect angel around teachers.

Sir Sprucewood looks at the two of us. "I don't know enough to tell who is lying. But I'm watching you, new kid..." Then, with sudden happiness, he says, "Anyway, time to go to the forest!"

I glare at Jeremy, who smiles deviously. I walk over to my friends.

"You okay, Eilsel?" Eoz asks.

"I'm fine. Let's go shoot some jerk—I mean targets," I snap.

Eoz looks concerned, but doesn't say anything. We continue into the forest in silence, until Sciprus notices me glaring at Jeremy.

"I'm guessing you met him." Sciprus points at Jeremy as he notes this.

"Yes." I pause. "I need to crush him in archery and make him pay."

Sciprus nods. "You do that. But be careful—he cheats. He will do anything to win," he warns.

Before I can tell Sciprus I'll be careful, he looks at Wren. There's this strange look in his eyes. At first I can't tell what it means, but after a while I realize he likes her.

I nudge Sciprus. "You liiiiiike her," I tease, elongating the 'i' in 'like'.

Sciprus glares at me and then hisses, "Shush! She'll hear!"

Wren looks at us curiously, then shrugs it off.

"Ask her out. You'll thank me later," I whisper.

"It's not like that! I can't just—what happens if she doesn't think of me that way? It could ruin our friendship," he stutters.

"If that happens, she doesn't deserve you. But besides, that's not going to happen," I assure him.

"I'll think about it," he says, and leaves it at that.

It's a good thing too, because we've arrived in a clearing with targets positioned around the edges.

"Right, I'm going to assign you partners and I'll see what you can do so far. Wren and Eoz, Sciprus and Roxy, Eilsel and Jeremy..."

I don't hear anything after that. I glare at the obnoxious jerk known as a human being. He glares back.

We head over to our target and grab our equipment. Jeremy pulls his bowstring back and nocks an arrow. Then he shoots. The arrow isn't dead center, but it's close.

"That's you. You're dead," he threatens.

I frown. This kid's worse than I thought.

"You're probably not that good, anyway. I bet you were lying about hunting live animals," Jeremy adds.

"We'll see." I step up to the target, pull my bowstring back, and nock an arrow.

I concentrate intensely and ignore Jeremy, who is jumping up and down and singing "Eilsel's a loser, Eilsel's a loser," so only I can hear.

I shoot, and the moment my arrow leaves the bow I close my eyes. I can hear a satisfying thwack that I know must be the arrow hitting the target. Jeremy stops singing. I open my eyes. In the middle of the target is a hole, and through it I can see the arrow I shot on the ground. For some reason, I fight the urge to howl in victory.

"And that," I say. "Is you."

THE ALLIANCE

EOZ PAWZORD

O n my way to school the next day it's cold and windy. My scarf keeps blowing in my face while we're walking.

"We have our test today. Did you guys study?" I ask, assuming Eilsel hasn't.

She still gets good grades and all, but sometimes I question her preparation skills.

"What test?" Eilsel asks.

"Seriously, the science test on tree growth! You didn't study?" Wren exclaims.

Eilsel rolls her eyes. "Of course I studied."

"Hey, what's with Eilsel?" Wren asks me.

"I don't know. She has some beef with some kid from school," I say.

"Oh," she replies.

8:29, right on time. I go into the school house and take a seat at my desk. Mrs. Lavourne is writing something on the blackboard, something for the test. Eilsel's seat is in the very back, while mine and Wren's are in the second row. Sciprus is somewhere in front of us.

"Okay, class, time for the test, take out your quills," the professor tells us. As she hands out the test, I go over the facts in my head.

Question 1: Name five kinds of trees with larch leaves.

I list five and go on to the next question. Eilsel keeps scrubbing her eraser on her paper. I don't think she studied. I look down and answer the next question. Another boy in my class is reading a book instead of taking the test. He's going to get in trouble.

"Okay class, ten minutes left." Mrs. Lavourne announces after about twenty minutes.

I finish my test and drop it at her desk.

"Okay, thank you, Eoz. You can wait in the hallway," she tells me.

I go outside and wait for my friends to finish. Shortly after, Wren joins me outside.

"How'd you do?" I ask Wren.

She shrugs. "I don't know, it was kind of easy."

"Yeah, I agree."

Some other kids in our class finish their tests and wait outside with us.

The Headmaster walks by and greets us. "Good morning, scholars."

Finally, Eilsel comes out of the classroom.

"How was it?" I ask.

She ignores me and walks to her next class.

"All right, students, it's time for lunch," the professor says.

We all walk single file into the cafeteria. Wren and I walk slowly having a conversation about our history paper that is due soon. A few boys behind us start muttering to themselves, but we just ignore them and keep walking.

Our lunch table is for four people: myself, Eilsel, Wren and Sciprus. Eilsel never shows. It's only been a couple days at Star Village Academy and Eilsel has already found a way to sneak off somewhere. When she returns, she looks like she has fought a Demon-Bear.

"Where'd you go?" I ask.

"Doesn't matter," she replies.

She gets her food and eats in silence.

In the middle of history, a man dressed in a red cloak and black hat comes into our classroom.

"Hello, are you Elizabeth Clark?" he grunts at our professor.

All the students peer at him suspiciously as he walks to the front of the room.

"Yes, I'm the history professor," she answers.

"Well, I need to have a word with you," he says, motioning Mrs. Clark over to his side.

I lean forward to listen.

"The schools are being put in danger. The war is yet to come and we need to keep the students safe. I'm a soldier for the Aurorans and I was sent to inform all the schools in this district," he informs Mrs. Clark, trying to keep his voice down but failing.

"What war?" she asks.

I look at Eilsel. Even though she has been distracted all day, she is managing to listen in on this.

"We are trying to not spread it to the general public yet, but we need to tell you. Two Fantastical children have just been discovered and are on the loose. They are very dangerous. In fact, they are the cause of this war," he answers.

Instantly, I know who they are talking about. Me and Eilsel. His words 'they are the cause of the war' ring in my ears. The four of us look at each other. What have we done?

The soldier moves on to the next classroom by the time the class period ends. We all huddle up outside of the classroom.

"We need to leave school now," Wren says, keeping her voice to a whisper.

"Okay, what if we try and escape through the garden door," Eilsel suggests.

Sciprus shakes his head. "No, the lunch ladies will see us."

I try to remember any escapes I read about in my books. They were all extremely hard or unrealistic. Then I get the answer.

"Guys. Look up!" I exclaim.

None of them look up; they all just stare.

"Oh c'mon, we don't have time for this." Wren says.

"No, really. Look up!" I reply.

Reluctantly, they all peer at the ceiling, and then Eilsel gasps. "Eoz, you may be right. This could work."

"Shhhh." I pull them into the janitor's closet where we can hide.

"Okay, everyone clear with the plan?" Sciprus asks.

I look around the group of us in the stinky room.

"Umm... one thing," Wren starts. "I have claustrophobia."

I bite my lip, and look at my watch. "Oh, boy. Okay, umm... Wren, you and I can go through the garden. The lunch lady is probably still on break, so we should have approximately four minutes."

"Okay sounds like a plan to me," Eilsel agrees.

"Okay, Sciprus, Eilsel, climb up into the vents. They should lead to the dumpster or something, and meet us there." Then, I turn to Wren and ask, "Ready?"

We scramble to the kitchen sink and slip underneath.

"Is anyone here?" I ask Wren.

She peeks out to look around. "Coast is clear."

We scurry out the door into the garden.

"The dumpster is not far from here," Wren reminds me.

We soundlessly run over to the dumpster to meet our friends and escape Star Village Academy.

Three dumpsters are lined up next to each other. The vent leads into the first dumpster. We walk over, crouching, to see if Sciprus and Eilsel are hiding inside. They aren't. Unfortunately, someone is here, though—the little old lunch lady taking out the trash.

"Do you—" Wren starts, but I clamp my hand over her mouth as soon as I see the lunch lady.

Too late.

"What are you two doing here? Shouldn't you be in class?" she questions.

"Yes ma'am," Wren mumbles.

"If there's no hall pass, then you have to be in class."

We both nod. That second, Eilsel and Sciprus roll out of the broken vent into the dumpster.

"Oh no, not you too," the lunch lady exclaims as she looks at our friends. "I'm taking you to the Headmaster."

We walk silently to the headmaster's office. The door is locked so we have to knock. They open it after a second.

"Hello Judith, what brings you here?" the Headmaster asks the lunch lady.

"These four tried to escape," she explained.

"What you did was very wrong. What was the meaning of this?"

We all stay silent. None of us are going to risk saying something we're gonna regret. Finally, the headmaster stops questioning us.

"Fine. What are your parents' names?" they ask.

We all look at one another and sadly shake our heads.

PURPOSEFUL EXPULSION

EILSEL PAWZORD

The headmaster eventually lets us out of their office, after much questioning. I think they ultimately realized that asking us who our parents are (were) would do no good. They seemed to notice this after a bit, and I guess they must feel sorry for us because they only gave us a warning.

The day is over now, and we walk back to the abandoned house the four of us were staying in. Wren and Sciprus have been here a lot longer than us, but they've been happy to share.

"We can't just leave, can we?" Sciprus asks finally, breaking the silence.

I nod, knowing he's referring to the school. I don't want to leave. Even though there are jerks at the Star Village Academy, there are amazing people too. Like Sciprus, Wren, and this girl named Roxy who is obsessed with all things fashion.

I was angry today, I'll admit. Madam Lavourne noticed something was wrong and said I could do the test tomorrow with no consequences after the headmaster gave us our warning. I suppose she must've pitied us, too. I know I can ace it tomorrow, after PE.

I know I had that victory against Jeremy on the first day of school, but after I learned about the PE tournament, it wasn't good enough. I know I have to beat him, so that's what I'm going to do tomorrow.

"Well." Wren pauses, as if deciding whether what she's about to say is semi-crazy. She continues, though. "We could get expelled."

And I'm right, her idea is crazy. But it warms me back up, makes me want to laugh again. I don't want to think about how we're the cause of—about what we learned at school today. It's bringing me down, and I don't want to think that all those people—*stop*. I need to stop. I take a deep breath and grin. Nobody needs to know how deeply I'm blaming all of this on myself. What I need to do is to continue on as though everything is normal.

"I know just how to get expelled," I say deviously.

Eoz looks concerned, and gives Wren "the look." Unspoken words are in that look, and those words are most likely "my sister has another crazy plan that's going to get us all expelled." I mean, that is the point, after all.

The only flaw of my plan is that I'm not going to get to retake the test. Even so, I might as well study after telling everyone the plan—which I know is going to be good.

* * *

It's the day. We arrive at school early so we can get the last bits of our plan down. When I say the last bit, Wren looks incredibly happy.

"Jeremy's always been a jerk. He can go and burn for all I care." Wren laughs. "Joking, joking!" she shouts when Sciprus gives her a look.

First period goes by in a blur. Not one of Jeremy's insults reach my ears, and I can tell this annoys him. His irritation is about the only thing interesting enough to hold my attention. All I can think about is our plan. Finally, *finally* Sir Sprucewood takes us to the grounds where we'll spring our trap.

"I will now remind you of your teams!" he booms, once we get there. "Jeremy, Lawson, Beatrice, Harrison, and Lynx make up team Monster-Hunters. The team that will be playing the Monster-Hunters for the championship is made up of Eilsel, Eoz, Sciprus, Wren, and Roxy. They are the Illusion-Mages." Sprucewood looks around. "Your fifth teammate is home sick, so you'll have to play with one less player. I'm sure you'll be fine, though!"

"Darn," I whisper to Eoz, quietly so Jeremy's team won't hear. "Roxy was the best at hiding our flag!"

Eoz shrugs. "We can still do this."

Sprucewood continues. "Interesting name choice, by the way. In the olden days, Illusion Mages were some of the most powerful—and feared—mages. They could make people see things that weren't there. Of course, they're all gone now. Ah, sorry for that short history lesson! Now, not all of you made it to the finals, but you still deserve mentions!"

I could've sworn Wren flinched when Sir Sprucewood started talking about the powerful and feared Illusion Mages. Her reaction was probably nothing, though.

"Right. On the Troutfish we have Benji, Kailash, Stella, Madeleine, Max, and Nicole."

Three boys and three girls wave their hands, though one boys' is held up by another.

"Then on the Fishtrout—oh, I see what you did there!—is Addison, Annabelle, Turner, Avery, and Morgan, and Flora."

Only one girl cheers. Another is clearly disappointed that her team has lost to the Monster-Hunters. A redhead is fighting with a boy who looked as though he could be her brother. Another girl is looking at her twin, who is on another team. The last girl, with hair so dark it looks black, is trying to hide the fact she's reading a book. It has an alicorn on its cover. I'll have to ask if I can borrow it... Oh wait, I'm trying to get expelled. Never mind!

"Now, for a reminder of the rules. There are two sides and two flags. But this is *not* capture the flag. It's a similar game, yes, but slightly different. You'll need to hide your flag at the beginning of the game, and once you've done that you'll need to find the other team's flag. Be warned, once you cross the border, the other team can shoot you—"

"What!? Shoot? Last time it was capture the flag, why are you changing the rules on us now?" one of Jeremy's friends shouts in outrage.

"Who said I couldn't?" Sprucewood asks innocently "We'll be able to tell you've been tagged when you've been colored with a paint hidden in the tips of the arrow. Don't worry, it won't kill you—maybe a bruise, sure, but nothing worse. You'll be out when that happens. Good luck!"

I nod my head and join Sciprus and Wren, Eoz right next to me.

"We don't have Roxy today," Sciprus states.

"Well, we knew that. How are we gonna hide our flag without them finding it? None of us had any good ideas last time," Wren scoffs in disdain.

Eoz looks similarly doubtful. I think for a moment, and eventually come up with something.

"I've got it!" I whisper loudly.

My friends turn to me.

"Go on," Sciprus prompts.

"He said it was shooting, right? Then we've got this. I'll be in a tree near the flag, and if anyone from that jerk's team gets close I'll shoot. Meanwhile, you guys can focus on the offense," I say.

Wren grins. "I think that might work!"

Sprucewood walks over to our team with the Monster-Hunters right behind him. He stops and our team and Jeremy's team look at each other. By look, I mean we glare.

Sir Sprucewood obviously notices this, as he starts talking hurriedly. "I want a good, fair game! Now, to your sides!"

He points at the Monster-Hunters who go to the right, and then at us, who go to the other side.

Bows and arrows full of paint lie waiting for us. I pick mine up, and the rest of the Illusion-Mages do too, so we can keep our strategy hidden. It would be a dead give away if only I picked up my stuff, after all.

We head into the forest, and I instantly feel at home. I remember hunting and sledding and doing all sorts of things in Peril Forest with Aikai and Eoz... but that's in the past now. I need to focus on the present, so that's what I'll do.

When we get to a circle of tall oak trees—hah, my studying paid off!—we stop, and everyone besides me puts their items down. I grab one of Eoz's arrows, and she looks at me curiously. I pry it open and paint blue waves and lightning bolts on the bow.

Eoz laughs. "Should've known."

I pull out five arrows. Black, brown, dark grey, grey, and white. Remembering some of Jeremy's previous insults, I exchange the grey arrow for a bright pink one. Wren and Eoz smile deviously, and even Sciprus laughs a bit.

"Jeremy will look pretty in pink," Wren chuckles.

"Exactly my point," I say.

We hide the flag right on top of some boulders. Our flag is grey, so it blends in well. I climb a tree and notch the black arrow. I know that jerk won't be the first one to come; he'll send his cronies after us first.

Sir Sprucewood's horn bellows through the air, signalling the start of the game. Sciprus, Wren, and Eoz stalk towards the border between our teams almost silently. I adjust my position in the tree so I'll be able to shoot the moment anyone comes near.

At least ten minutes pass without any movement. I can hear yelling in the distance, presumably from either Jeremy's team or the kids watching. Finally, I hear a rustle in the bushes. A boy comes out. He has pale blond hair and blue eyes, so I can tell it's Lynx. He doesn't like Jeremy much, but since he's a bit of a loner he was chosen last and shoved onto the jerk's team. I feel bad for him, but I'm still going to do my job.

I pull my bowstring with the dark grey arrow back, aim, and fire. It hits Lynx's head, so not the most accurate shot, and splatters his hair with black paint. Lynx looks up and smiles at me.

'Thanks!' He mouths. 'My parents won't let me get my hair dyed, so this is great!'

Lynx turns and walks towards the border, which I can't actually see. I hear shouts of "Lynx is out!"

I smile. One down, four to go. I notch the brown arrow. Jeremy won't come yet, but soon. Soon he will be splattered in bright, bright, pink, which is his least favorite color. That's probably the only thing we have in common.

I don't have to wait long for the next person, or should I say people. Beatrice and Harrison, who are cousins, come out around the bush on either side. Harrison points at the flag and the two of them immediately run at it. I shoot Harrison and then notch the white arrow. Beatrice almost gets to the flag before I get her.

Harrison sees me and nods, but Beatrice looks right over me.

"Ugh! Who got us?" she yells and stomps her foot.

Harrison and Beatrice walk away and—Jeremy! Out of nowhere is Jeremy!

He grabs the flag and starts running for the border. I jump out of the tree with the pink arrow and my bow and race after him, slightly stunned from jumping from the height.

Jeremy has a head start, but years of running through the woods chasing animals has made me an okay runner. That's not to say I like doing it—I prefer ambushes like the way I caught Lynx. The point is, I should be able to catch up pretty fast.

The trees and underbrush seem to fly by as I run to tag Jeremy, but wait. Wait, wait, wait. I can't believe I forgot! This isn't normal capture the flag. I have to shoot him. I stop running as we near the border, and hide in a bush. This may seem stupid, but I know Jeremy won't just step over the line. He'll make a show out of it.

"Hah! Given up, have you?" he laughs.

I stay quiet, not wanting to give away my position. I prepare to shoot, but as I aim, I see Eoz running towards the border with the Monster-Hunters' flag in hand. I grin. Jeremy doesn't have his bow, nor his arrows.

However unlikely it may be, the King of the Jerks might decide to book it and step over the line to victory. I can't let that happen. I want to win. I pull the bowstring back and fire. Jeremy is covered from head to toe with bright pink paint. The rest of our class bursts out laughing, and I step out from the bush just as Eoz brings the flag to our side.

"Pink, pink, Jeremy looks pretty in pink!" the class chants.

The jerk known as Jeremy practically turns red. Sprucewood is attending to Lawson, who apparently fell out of a tree because of 'a ghost' when Wren, Sciprus, and Eoz got near his flag. Jeremy apparently doesn't care that all of the sixth level is watching.

"What?! No! The Illusion Mages didn't win, we did!" the boy who I have grown to know and hate shouts to the rest of our class.

Jeremy seems to be grasping at straws, trying to find something to insult us with. I assume he does, because he looks directly at me and starts yelling.

"What a stupid team name, anyway! You know, when the Illusion Mages were around, they were allies with the Fantasticals! Is that what you want? For us to live in peace with those *monsters*? There are two on the loose right now—"

Jeremy is interrupted by Lynx, the kid whose hair I unintentionally helped dye earlier. "I-isn't that a bit overkill, Jeremy? The ones running around are still kids; a soldier who was here a little ago told me that. H-how do we know that they're monsters? What if some of them are nice?"

"They're obviously not, you idiot! The Fantasticals are all bloodthirsty animals who deserve what they're getting! They're not people!" Jeremy screams.

Eoz looks pale, and all I want to do is run away, right back to Peril Forest.

But I can't. I know I can't. This is Jeremy, of all people. Am I really going to let that guy get to me? No, of course not. What I'm going to do next is going to get me expelled, and probably the rest of my team minus Roxy as well. But hey, that's the point. So I walk up to him and punch him right in his stupid face.

Should I have done it? No.

Am I going to apologize? No.

But did it feel good? *Definitely.*

THE WARNING

EOZ PAWZORD

"We're leaving!" I scream in Eilsel's ear.

"Yeah, wake up sleepy head!" Wren snickers.

Eilsel gets out of the blankets and ties her hair up with some twine. "Okay, we can go now."

"Boy am I starving!" I say.

"We don't have time for hunting, but there are some strawberries in that bush," Wren explains.

I walk over and pick a few berries. A sweet fuzzy feeling warms me up as I eat them. Almost like back in the Peril Forest.

"Ready?" Sciprus asks.

"Yeah, let's go."

I pull my hood over my head. The air is cold and tinted with the morning sunlight. We have a long journey to Scalia, and an even longer one if we get lost.

"So, how do we know which way Scalia is?" Eilsel asks Sciprus.

"Well, I do know that Scalia is south and moss grows north," he answers.

Eilsel nods.

"Okay, so all we need to do is find some moss!" Wren realizes.

We walk around the woods brushing snow off the tree trunks.

"Any luck?" I call out.

"No!" Everyone replies in unison.

I go from tree to tree brushing snow until my white mittens are soaking wet.

"Hey, I think I found something!" Eilsel cries.

We all rush over to her and huddle around the tree.

"Is it moss?" Eilsel asks.

"It sure looks like it!" Sciprus announces.

So we begin our journey in the opposite direction of the moss.

"Hey this isn't so bad," Wren says.

"Yeah, I guess the sun came out a bit," I agree.

Eilsel takes an arrow out of her hunting bag and starts jabbing trees with it along the way.

"Cut it out," I say, annoyed from the crunching noise of the arrow going through the bark.

"Fine," Eilsel replies, putting her bow back in her hunting bag. "You don't have to be so grumpy," I hear her mutter.

Once the snow has melted even more and there are more valleys and ridges, we know we've entered the third biggest territory—Home of the Prowls. Some cows are grazing on the side of some hills. A small neighborhood fills part of the plains at the foot of the hills with the cows. It seems to be humanoid goats living there.

* * *

After a few hours or so of endless walking, the sun peaks high in the sky and clouds float in around it.

"Let's get some lunch," Eilsel says as she tightens the strap on her hunting bag.

"Yeah, those strawberries weren't very filling. Let's get some real food," Wren agrees.

"Okay, you and Eilsel can go hunt something while Eoz and I go find a shelter," says Sciprus.

I nod. "Okay, see you guys later."

"Check out this cave!" I exclaim, motioning Sciprus towards me.

We enter it cautiously, staying on our toes just in case.

"It doesn't look deep, and there doesn't seem to be any tunnels. This place seems pretty good," he informs me.

"Let's gather some firewood," I say after we explore the small cave a little more.

As I expected, there aren't any logs just cut up into perfect firewood, so I just collect twigs and sticks instead.

Once we return, Sciprus and I throw the sticks into a messy pile.

"This big one looks good to start the fire, and this rock seems good for the rubbing," I say, picking up a stick and stone.

Sciprus agrees and gathers more rocks for the outside of the fire. After only a few short minutes, we were ready to start the fire.

"You really need to rub it there," I say to Sciprus.

"Yeah, I know," he replies, rubbing the stick against the rock. His ears are red as a tomato.

"Sciprus, Eoz! Where are you?" Wren calls from somewhere outside of the cave. I'd recognize her voice anywhere.

"We're in here!" I reply, standing outside of the cave.

"Okay! We're coming."

Late at night we are all still awake. None of us could even dream of sleeping given the circumstances we have.

"I've never traveled this far," Sciprus says looking around the cave.

Wren smiles. "That's what's fun. We don't know what's coming next."

I listen to their conversation, but try to concentrate on sketching a map into a rock.

"Guys, check this out!" I motion to my friends to come over.

Since the sky is so dark, it's hard to see much of anything.

"Is that a map?" Wren asks.

"Yeah, sort of, it's all the places we've been, starting at the Starlight Festival." I show them the school and the abandoned treehouse and the things we've hunted along the way.

Everyone adds other details they remember, and finally the map is complete.

"We should try and get some sleep," Eilsel reminds us.

"Yeah, it's a busy day tomorrow," Sciprus agrees.

We all lie on the dirt floor of the cave, using rocks as pillows, trying to get as comfortable as we can.

"Good night," I chime.

Everyone answers good night, our voices echoing against the walls.

* * *

The next morning we come across a herd of brown, furry animals.

"Are those monkeys?" Eilsel screams, pointing at them.

They are sitting in a tree sharpening sticks with their teeth.

"Yep, those are monkeys," Wren assures her.

We slowly inch away, staying on our toes. Eilsel clenches her bow in her palm, getting ready to pounce.

Suddenly, a stick snaps under one of our shoes. All the monkeys turn their heads, every single one of them staring at us. Well, besides one, he kind of had his own thing going. The biggest one crawls forward. He stands up and howls so loud I bet you the Peril Forest could have heard him. All the monkeys jump up and turn to attack. They are throwing their sticks and carving new ones before we can even comprehend what is happening.

"Charge!" Wren screams, running at the herd.

Eilsel draws her bow and Sciprus makes a slingshot from some things he finds on the ground. Monkeys are going down bleeding and whimpering aloud. Their sticks do hurt if they hit you at the right angle.

"Eoz, hurry! Do something!" Eilsel exclaims.

I tear a dead branch off a tree and swing it around like a caveman. More monkeys fall to the ground, leaving a trace of monkey smell from where they were huddled.

"Okay, lets go!" I announce, leading everyone out of the opening of the trees.

"Eoz, I didn't like the looks of those monkeys," Wren tells me on the walk out of the Prowl territory.

"Yeah, I'm not entirely sure if those were even monkeys."

Sciprus knits his eyebrows, "What do you mean they aren't monkeys?"

"Well, it was hard to tell from far away, but they all seemed to have perfect red eyes, almost *too* perfect." Wren pauses. "I believe that those monkeys are *Demon*-Monkeys, very similar to the Demon-Bear."

Out of the corner of my eye, I can see Eilsel shivering at the mention of the historic Demon-Bear.

ILLUSIONS

EILSEL PAWZORD

After the Demon-Monkey incident, we decide we need to move faster if we want to make it to the Scalians ahead of the combined Auroran-Flare army. So we get less sleep, and the morale isn't great. Everyone is always in a bad mood. Now, even when I make the 'Jeremy looked pretty in pink' joke, no one laughs.

I'm sure everyone would be a lot happier if we knew we're ahead of the opposing army, but there's no way we can find out. So instead, we stick to plodding on in silence as fast as we can. I'm getting seriously bored of it. I wish someone would just talk so it wouldn't be so quiet, but my prayer goes unanswered.

After a bit, it starts to get dark. The sun falls behind the valleys and forests that we've passed, including the outskirts of Prowl Territory where we fought the so-called monkey-things. Wren finally speaks, and under all the mud and dirt on my face, I beam.

"So, where are we going to stay tonight?" she asks.

I look around the area. It wouldn't be easy to defend, as it is very open with little to no hiding spots. A mountain that we know we'll have to climb eventually looms in front of us, but we would be unable to now that it's so dark.

I remember the terrain we passed previously, and it won't work for a camp either. I sigh. It looks like we have two options. We could try to climb the mountain now, or we could stay here in this incredibly defenseless clearing.

While I stand here thinking, I start to hear something. It sounds almost like footsteps, a lot of footsteps.

"Did you hear that?" I ask urgently.

"No, but what did you hear?" Eoz wonders aloud.

I listen intensely again. The footsteps seem to be getting closer. I try to remember what Aikai taught me all those weeks ago...he didn't have much time to teach us. I wish we could have learned more. Currently, all I know how to do is see in the dark when I want to, which is more subconscious than I'd like. I can also smell much better than the average human, but I really have to concentrate for that. Also, I guess I can hear a little better too.

If we'd had more time, if that person hadn't seen Eoz flying... I could be so much better at this. Maybe then I'd be more prepared for what's happening now. Maybe then we wouldn't have had to leave. I guess I miss Aikai more than I realized.

Oh, no. Oh no, oh no, oh no.

Aikai told us to hide, not go off warning the Scalians! He thinks we're still somewhere near Peril Forest, so when he searches for us he'll assume the worst. I can't believe that I forgot about this! But we can't turn back now. Maybe somehow we can get a message to him?

Agh, I need to concentrate. I can't let my mind wander.

Right, I should be able to identify what I hear if I can smell it too. Aikai said it would feel almost like an instinct or gut feeling, and that if I practiced I could get better at identification. I haven't had much time to practice, but whatever is marching our way could be dangerous. I need to know what it is.

I concentrate as hard as I can and then take a sniff of the air. It's very musty and I can smell a fresher breeze in the direction of the mountain. I focus my sense of smell on where I heard the footsteps.

I definitely smell something. It has this dirty taint to it, kind of like us but slightly cleaner. I think for a moment. Jjust like Aikai said I would, I know what it is, but I need to act fast.

"Soldiers! We need to find cover!" I shout as loud as I can without alerting the soldiers to our presence.

Eoz's eyes go wide. I would tell her to fly up and check if I was right, but we have no time.

Sciprus starts jumping up and down. "Over here!" he screams.

We rush over to where he is currently giddy with excitement.

"I found a cave!" Sciprus says happily.

We all rush inside, and just as I file in, rocks fall over the entrance.

Wren looks pale. "We're trapped!"

"We're not," Sciprus says.

We all turn toward him.

"This isn't like the cave we camped out in before the monkey incident," he says. "There are tunnels... In fact, I reckon we could just go straight under the mountain. We won't need to climb it after all!"

I smile in the darkness.

"That just might work!" Eoz whispers, still quiet.

The soldiers are probably right outside the cave, but I'm too tired to check on their location.

Wren notices this. "Eilsel, we need to keep moving. You can't fall asleep now."

I yawn, exhausted, but still nod at her statement.

"What are we going to do about how dark it is, though?" Eoz asks.

I look up in surprise. "It isn't dark."

My friends turn to look at me.

"Uh, yeah, it is," Wren says worriedly. "Maybe you should get some rest, Eilsel."

"Wait, no! She's right, *it isn't dark*," My twin sister whisper-shouts.

"What do you mean?" Sciprus asks.

"Well, I can barely see anything, but Eilsel's some type of wolf. Of course she'd be able to see in the dark!"

I smile. Finally, this whole Fantastical thing is paying off. Previously, it's caused us nothing but trouble, but now I can see that it's honestly fun being a Fantastical. There's so many things we can do now that we couldn't before. This makes me wonder, though. Why do humans think that our kind are monsters? If we're so helpful... but that's a topic for another day. I refocus my mind on the situation at hand.

Wren grins, even though I'm probably the only one who can see her smile.

"But what about you guys? I can't exactly hold all your hands and walk forward aimlessly," I say sadly.

"You won't have to," Sciprus says quietly.

He walks over to Wren, bumping into the wall as he does so. He nudges her, and Wren pales.

"He's right," she whispers, as if hoping she could turn invisible.

I look at Wren curiously.

"I'm an Illusion Mage. That's the reason I ran away. My family hates magic, and they say so very often. Knowing that I was part of those 'Magic-User Lunatics' that my family so often cursed, I had to get away. I did have a step-brother who cared for me, though. I feel bad for leaving him alone with our family. They keep telling him he needs to join the army and 'prove he's a man' or something like that. He's more a man than of any of them, far more than my step-father, even. He was always very opposed to fighting, and he taught me that I should never use violence if there was a way I could work a problem out with words.

"Most of the time I didn't listen to him. I got into several fights at Sciprus' old school. Eventually, I decided I would leave, that I couldn't take it anymore. I would start a new life somewhere I could be happy. I planned to leave alone, but Sciprus showed up that same night and told me he was going to run away and that he had come to say good-bye. We ended up running away together. We moved to a new town, and survived with money my step-brother had given me. He told me it was only for emergencies. Once I could've sworn I saw him in a soldier uniform... but it couldn't have been him. He never would've joined the army, and besides I think I see him everywhere sometimes."

I stare at Wren in shock. I didn't expect this. Now so many things make sense. How she flinched whenever the Illusion Mages were brought up, why she didn't like how Sciprus made our team name the Illusion Mages. Even the ghost that the kid saw during our Capture the Flag round where I punched Jeremy in the face and got us all expelled when our whole team refused to apologize... that was Wren.

She looks so sad, now. I shoot a look at Sciprus, trying to say something along the lines of 'You knew?' but he can't see me.

Wren starts talking again, stating how she can help, "I can use my powers to help you all see in the dark. I would need Eilsel to describe everything she can see right now in clear detail, since she can see fine right now, and then I can light it up. The downside is that everything will still be dark for me, because as an Illusion Mage I see through illusions of all kinds, even my own. I've been practicing simple things like this, so it shouldn't be too hard or draining for me."

I nod.

"I think it's amazing that you can do that, Wren," Sciprus says, with a quiet smile.

If this weren't such a bad situation I would almost be cheering, because Sciprus and Wren would be awesome together, but I stay silent.

"Yeah!" Eoz and I whisper simultaneously. It must be a twin thing.

"Thanks, guys. Now Eilsel, what do you see?" Wren asks, returning to her normal upbeat self.

I tell her what I see, describing each crack in the wall in detail. Wren nods along then scrunches up her face in intense concentration. Finally, she snaps her fingers.

"Now that was cool! It's basically as light as day!" Eoz gasps.

Wren smiles. "Right, it's still super dark for me, so maybe I could—this is kind of embarrassing—hold someone's hand?" she suggests, turning bright red.

I look at Sciprus. 'Now is your chance!' I mouth to him.

Eoz can clearly see and understand what I'm saying, but since it's still dark for Wren, she can't.

The red-headed boy shakes his head as fast as possible, so I jump into action. I am not letting him shy out of this again. If he likes her, he needs to find some way to show it.

"Sciprus will do it," I tell Wren, grinning evilly.

Eoz catches on to my plan. He must understand that Sciprus likes Wren.

"Oh okay, thanks Sciprus," Wren says gratefully.

Sciprus glares at Eoz and me. He takes Wren's hand, and we start walking through the twisting caverns. Every so often the green-eyed girl who I have come to know as a great friend asks me to describe the area again. Eoz's green eyes flicker over the cave with a happy sparkle. She's probably thinking the same thing as me. We're making much better time than we would've going over the mountains, and that by itself is truly amazing. I'm still really tired, though.

We eventually come to a giant cave full of stalagmites and... bones. I gulp. I don't think bones are a good sign.

"Uhh...Wren? It's dark again." Eoz says at normal volume since we're far away enough from the soldiers.

"That's strange. I'm still using my powers... huh." Wren says, clearly puzzled.

"I can still see things. There-there are a lot of bones on the ground..." I trail off because I hear something.

Instantly, I know what it is. It's something I had hoped to never hear again, something that has haunted my nightmares for years. I look up, hoping with all I have that I won't see what I know I will see.

Two piercing red eyes. That settles it, I know what's there. I-it's supposed to be an illusion, but it looks so real... I step on one of the bones. My foot doesn't go through it like it would a normal illusion. Oh no. Oh no, oh no, oh no.

Aikai was wrong. The Demon-Bear in front of us is very real and very angry. I need to warn my friends, but it's like no sound comes out.

Finally, a peep comes out of my mouth. "D-d-Demon-Bear. Real."

Eoz's eyes go wide. "Oh no, oh no... Eilsel, you're the only one who can see it. It's too dark for us... you need to—"

The bear charges straight at us, and I try to take out my hunting knife or *something* that could help us but, but.. .it's like I'm in that tree again. It's coming, and I can't get away. *I can't get away.*

All that exhaustion from earlier comes rushing back, and my fear heightens it. I've failed. We've come so far, and now it's my fault that we're all going to die here. It's my fault. The Demon-Bear gets closer and then all

I see is darkness.

BIRD CALL

EOZ PAWZORD

The fear rings through my head. Even if it wasn't me who fought the Demon-Bear a few years ago I still feel the pain almost like twin telepathy. The Demon-Bear charges at me and I barely get away. While doing so I trip on a rock. Blood drips from my forehead and shoulder, but I try to ignore the pain. Wren and Sciprus are hiding behind a rock, and Eilsel's knocked out body is lying in a corner.

"We need a plan!" Once again, I look around the cave seeking an answer. "Sciprus run! It's gonna throw a rock at you!"

He scurries out of the way just in time. "I'm coming to you!"

"Do you have a plan?" Sciprus asks me.

"I think so, but I'm going to need your help," I reply.

He nods. "What do you need?"

I duck down lower hoping the Demon-Bear hasn't spotted us yet.

"Okay, I'm going to fly above its head without it seeing me. Then you are going to throw a rock at it to make it mad. And finally I'll drop a rock on its head. Hopefully it will knock him unconscious for at least long enough to get out of here."

Sciprus thinks about my plan for a minute but then agrees. "Okay, it's a long shot, but let's give it a try."

I take off my cloak and my watch, putting it under a rock. It's the first time my wings have been free in so long.

"Okay, I'm going." I say.

I begin to flap my wings and think about everything that Aikai has taught me. Once I realized that I was off the ground, it was easy as pie. It felt like nothing was happening, just me and the sky.

I wave my hand, motioning for Sciprus to throw the rock. When it hits the Demon-Bear, it screams in anger. I'm just above him holding another huge rock. Sciprus runs around the cave, trying to provoke the bear.

"Now!" he cries.

I drop the rock on his head, and it rolls down to his nose and makes a piercing shriek as it hits the ground. I fly back to the ground and hide behind the rock with Wren.

At first the Demon-Bear seems to be unconscious. Its shiny red eyes are rolled back and it is flat as a pancake. But after only a few seconds, it rises from the ground and roars so loud the entire cave vibrates.

"Run!" I shriek at the top of my lungs.

But there is nowhere to go. We are cornered with the bear blocking the entrance of the cave.

"I'm not sure we're making it out alive," Sciprus whispers.

"We will," Wren says. "I know we will."

I stand toward the backside of the Demon-Bear, and begin throwing sticks and rocks. Sciprus is on the left side trying to stab it with one of Eilsel's abandoned arrows.

"Wren! Get out of the way!" I yell, even though she's only a few feet away from me.

"Guys, I think I know how to defeat it!" Wren exclaims, ignoring my instructions.

Momentarily, a bear paw whacks Wren to the floor.

"What is it?" I ask her as she scrambles to her feet.

She shakes her head, "No time to explain."

She runs to the other side where Eilsel is lying and grabs her bow and arrow from her satchel. Wren squats down under a rock and puts the arrow into the bow. I watch her draw back as I have with Eilsel so many times. She releases her arrow, and it flies into the heart of the Demon-Bear.

The bear isn't bleeding. It just falls to the ground and whimpers like a puppy. Wren had perfect aim. I didn't know she could hunt that well. When we all turn around the bear, disintegrates with a snap of a finger.

"You did it. You defeated a Demon-Bear!" I say with glee.

"I still don't understand how you knew it would do that if you hit it in the heart," Sciprus says.

"I'm not really sure to be honest. I kind of just knew," she says.

I look at Eilsel, who is just waking up. "I'm just glad we didn't die back there."

Everyone nods in agreement, though Eilsel is a little slow on the uptake.

"So, what happened back there?" Eilsel asks cluelessly.

I shake my head. "Not much, besides the fact that Wren killed a Demon-Bear."

"Hey, that's really cool," Eilsel replies.

Even though I know she was trying to sound nice, I could hear the tiniest bit of bitterness in her voice.

"Technically, the Demon-Bear isn't dead yet," Wren says.

We all look up at her, alarmed.

"What do you mean?" Sciprus asks.

"Well, you know how all humanoids die twice?" she asks.

We nod.

"Well, that Demon-Bear hadn't died yet, so it was still a real bear—not an illusion."

Eilsel's face turns red. "I thought that they were all illusions."

Wren shakes her head. "No, they are just like normal humanoids. For example, when you die, being the Fantastical that you are, you will return to magic, or *become* magic. However when a non-fantastical humanoid dies for the first time, they would become just the normal version of their animal, like the kinds we hunt."

Eilsel and I had known that, but we hadn't known that Demon-Bears weren't always illusions. Why had Aikai never told us that? Was he trying to hide it from us?

"So yes, that Demon-Bear hadn't died before, meaning it will come back to life, appearing as a ghost, very soon," Wren explains.

We nod.

"And may I ask how you know that?" Eilsel asks.

"Wren tends to know stuff. You'll get used to it," Sciprus tells us.

ILLEGAL CROSSINGS

EILSEL PAWZORD

Demon-Bears are no fun. Seriously, they aren't. Especially when they try to kill you and narrowly fail to do so.

Needless to say, after Wren killed the Demon-Bear we hightailed right on out of that cave. Wren's illusion magic had exhausted her, so everyone trailed behind me while I talked about everything and anything so they knew where I was. Eventually, we made it out of that cave, and we did indeed make faster time than we would've going over that mountain.

As it turns out, we were a *lot* closer to the Scalian Swamp than initially expected. Plains and valleys turned into trees and murky brown water, which leaves us right where we are now.

"I think we're getting close to the border," Eoz states. "It looks a lot more like a swamp."

I nod my head in agreement. Eoz stops walking for a moment, then sketches something on our make-shift map. She's been extremely attached to that thing ever since we made it on our first night in Prowl territory.

We keep walking on and on. I would say it's incredibly boring, but it really isn't. There are so many things I've never seen before, and I want to know what all of it is.

I walk up to Sciprus. "What's that?" I point at something that looks like a cross between a frog and a snake.

"It's a salamander," Sciprus says, looking at me smugly.

He finally knows something I don't about nature, but I'm not going to let him savor the moment.

"Well, what's that?" I question, and run over to a big green rock.

Sciprus' eyes flash over it curiously. "Err, maybe if I get a closer look I'll be able to tell."

The joke's on him, I know exactly what that 'big green rock' is. It's an alligator, and a good sized one at that. I know the gator won't do anything to my friend unless he provokes it, because it looks old and tired despite it's large body mass.

Sciprus walks towards the alligator and pokes it. I cringe. Eoz and Wren look back on us and stop, not knowing what's about to happen. Actually, I think Wren does, but she knows I'm not going to let Sciprus get eaten. Not when he still hasn't professed his love to her... I gotta make that happen soon.

The gator's eyes open slowly, and when it sees a boy with fiery red hair standing in a sea of greens and browns, it opens its jaws. Sciprus shrieks and runs the heck away from the creature like a mouse from, well... me.

I run to my sister and friend and burst out laughing. When Sciprus finally catches up to us, he glances at me accusingly.

"You knew that was a crocodile!" he says angrily.

"It was an alligator, actually." I chuckle.

"I could've been eaten!" he shouts.

I can't help laughing. "Nah, you wouldn't have. That thing is so old it could probably only barely catch a frog, much less you."

Eoz is trying to radiate seriousness, but one look at Sciprus's disgruntled and semi-angry face has her struggling to stop from grinning.

"Well, I forgive you," Sciprus admits.

"I needed forgiving?" I say in mock surprise.

My friend rolls his eyes, knowing he can't win, and even Wren's green eyes flicker with laughter.

Our good mood is soon ruined the moment we climb up over a ridge. An extremely large platoon of Auroran and Flare soldiers is marching about below. A wide river, which water is rushing through furiously, is right on the opposite side of their camp.

We had seen a map of the Scalian border while studying at the human school, so we knew that if we crossed the river we'd be on Scalian territory.

"You know how to swim, right?" I ask.

I know Eoz does from the days she had spent in the stream while I hunted, but I'm not sure about Sciprus and Wren. Thankfully, they nod, affirming that they do indeed know how to swim.

There still stands the challenge of getting through the soldier base. It's pocketed with trees and little ponds that make the camp seem a lot more homey than it actually is.

"Well, how are we going to get through?" Sciprus wonders aloud.

"We'll need to sneak in and sneak out," Eoz practically commands.

"Well, we'll need to do it soon, before the fog clears out and we become easily visible," Wren notes.

Eoz has copied some of what was on her map onto some mud with a stick. It isn't a particularly good drawing, unlike her map, which she used the utmost detail upon.

She points to some scratchy marks. "We can climb down from the ridge here, onto that tree—"

"Just like spying in Peril Forest, huh?" I interject.

Eoz smiles for a moment, then continues. "We can jump from that tree into that pond. I can see an underwater tunnel that comes out from it and pops up into that bigger pond by that big black tent. From there, we can swim one more time into the river, then paddle our way across. Does that sound good?" she finishes.

"Sir, yes sir!" Sciprus jokes.

Wren rolls her eyes. "Yeah, it works. Let's do this before the sun comes up. My mage powers aren't strong enough to fool so many people."

And with that, we start to move. I climb down first, because apparently night vision is the same thing as fog vision. Helpful, right? The last time I used this power was probably when that stupid bear attacked us, but before that was when... Aikai taught us. I miss him a lot sometimes, even though I try not to think about him. Did he make it to the Owl-Aviaren's secret place? I hope he's not looking for us now. He told us to hide, but that's not really what we did. In fact, we're kinda about to walk into the camp of our enemy... Well, can't think about that now, no matter how much it nags at me.

Pebbles skid off the ledges I step on, and I'm suddenly glad I've had so much practice with this sort of thing. Eventually, I'm close enough to the tree that I can probably jump onto it. The ledge I'm standing on is just wide enough for me to get a few steps of propulsion.

"Hurry up, Eilsel!" My twin mutters from above, not knowing that I can hear her.

I back up so that my back is pressing against the wall, and then I take one step, two steps, jump! I must have leaped a little too hard, because I slam into the tree's trunk and barely manage to get onto the branch without falling off. Wren comes down next, and her jump is a little too short. I grab her hand and pull her up, pushing the edge of the branch down so it doesn't poke me. When I release it, it snaps right up in my face.

"Ouch!" I yelp, then immediately clamp my hand over my mouth.

I can feel a cut on my forehead oozing blood. When Eoz gets onto the tree, we become quite crowded sitting up here.

She takes one look at my forehead and practically snickers, "Eilsel, proud hunter, beaten by a tree branch."

"Hey, this hurts!" I groan.

Now... into the water I go." I sigh, knowing the water will be freezing and dirty.

I leap down from the tree into the water after making sure there aren't any soldiers patrolling nearby. I was right, the water is cold, but surprisingly it doesn't look that dirty. My feet can't touch the ground, so I start treading water. Soon, the rest of my friends plunge into the water around me, making little splashes that soak me all over again.

Wren gestures for me to swim through the tunnel, but I shake my head.

"No way. Eoz, this is your plan, you go first," I say, looking at my sister.

Eoz actually looks pleased that I called this out as her plan. She takes a deep breath and swims through the tunnel as quickly and quietly as possible.

Wren follows her, and then it's just me and Sciprus.

"You know, you gotta make a move if you want her to notice you," I say, grinning, then I dive under the water without giving him a chance to respond.

The water is dark, and I hit my head on the rock more than a few times before I pop up. I hit my head—yet again—on the ceiling. Thankfully, there's enough space to come up for air. Sadly, none of us have water-breathing powers, so oxygen is a must have. Eoz is next to me.

"I thought this tunnel led to another pond!" I whisper-shout.

"Yeah, well, Wren isn't here, so I assume we just took a wrong turn," Eoz retorts.

I look around. It's still as bright as day for me, what with my night vision. I finally learned how to turn it off sometimes, because it can get seriously annoying when it's dark and you're trying to sleep. I sniff the air. It's quite stale, but I can detect a few traces of fresher stuff coming from a small bit ahead.

"I smell something. The air here won't last forever, so follow me," I say.

Eoz looks at me uneasily, but she dives under the water behind me. It's too bad she doesn't have night vision, but she does have this weird sky vision thing.

We discovered it on our first night of training with Aikai, right after Eoz learned how to fly. She mentioned that she could see the ground perfectly fine, even though she was so high up. It did help that it was a full moon that night. When she fought the Demon-Bear in the cave it was still really dark for her, so we can assume that certain conditions have to be met for this 'sky vision' to come into play.

As it turns out, I was correct. We come up into another dark roof, and I'm about to say we should just turn around when Eoz notes that it isn't a cave roof. She pulls herself out of this hole and then hoists me up after her. We look around. I wonder where we... Oh no! This is a soldier tent.

"Eoz, we're in one of their tents!" I whisper.

She looks at me, eyes wide. But we're not alone here.

A tired voice croaks, "You, you're not Scalians... You should kill me now. I already told you vile *soldiers* that I'm not going to tell you *anything*."

I look at Eoz, and she looks back at me.

"Uhh, we're not soldiers," Eoz says timidly.

"Wait... are you here to rescue me? I knew they'd send someone! Even if you look a bit young, and aren't Scalians, you can save me! I'm Ruben, by the way. Anyway, see that key over there, on the tent door? They leave it there to taunt me, knowing I can't get it. But it unlocks my chains."

Wow, talk about a mood swing. But I still walk over to the key and untie it from the door. Then I walk over to the captured Scalian.

I can tell he's a Scalian because of two very obvious things. A, his hands are webbed. B, his eyes are similar to a tree frog. They're large and orange, with a little slit of black in them. I set to work and quickly unlock his chains.

"Wow, that was pretty fast for a human like you. Thank you, and how'd you do that?" Ruben asks.

I don't look at Eoz, because I've deducted that this guy is a frog-type Scalian, and frogs have the unique ability to see colors in the dark.

I don't know what to say, but thankfully, Eoz jumps in for me. "She's just always had a good sense of vision."

"Ah, okay. Don't talk, do you?" Ruben wonders aloud.

"No, I talk," I say.

"Don't talk often, then," he revises.

I nod. He's semi-right. I don't speak much when I'm around strangers that I don't think I can instantly trust. But when I'm around people I know and trust, I barely ever shut up.

"Follow us. We know a way out of here," Eoz says.

"Oh, goody! Lead the way!" Ruben crows.

I fall in line behind Eoz, with Ruben behind me. We step into the water, and eventually we find a hole just wide enough for us to go through. When we do, Sciprus and Wren are waiting for us.

"What took you so long?" Wren demands.

"We just rescued a Scalian prisoner," Eoz states and gestures at Ruben.

Sciprus nods. "Well, now we need to get out of here. Once the soldiers check his cell and see he's missing, they'll be on high alert."

With that, we quickly paddle across the pond to the tunnel that leads to the river. We swim across it, the rushing water almost sweeping us away. We crawl out of the river so as not to be seen by those on the other side of the banks, then run a while away. Finally, the five of us collapsed in a clearing. The sun begins to come out, and it dries us up slightly.

"You know, I don't think you actually came to rescue me. It wasn't your main objective," Ruben says.

Eoz nods at his statement, and her green eyes twinkle. "We're here to join the Scalians' army and help them fight the Auroran-Flare army."

I'm honestly shocked. That's not what we came here to do. We were going to warn them about how the Flares and Aurorans had joined forces. But Sciprus and Wren are nodding along with this, and we get up to continue walking to the Scalians' town without an objection from anyone.

Did Sciprus and Wren know Eoz wanted to do this? And if so, why wouldn't Eoz tell me? And so, the first seeds of distrust are sown between me and my sister. I have a horrible feeling that this is only the beginning.

THE SCALIAN SWAMP

EOZ PAWZORD

At last we have made it to Scalia. The unfamiliar smell of mud and dew fills the air. Plants cover the buildings in the small village, and the houses are halfway submerged in the swamp.

"Well, here we are, in the great old town of Scalia," Ruben says.

"They sure don't call it the swamp city for nothing," Eilsel adds.

"I should probably get back home, but thanks for everything," Ruben says.

"Okay, we'll see you later," Wren replies.

When we walk into town our shoes get very wet and muddy. A baker on a corner and a scroll boy on another. It is a very quaint little town. A kid about our age comes up to us.

"Are you guys tourists?" he asks.

"Yeah, kind of," I admit.

"So, what brings you here?" he asks, eyeing the scratches and scars on our faces.

"We're here to fight in the war," Wren informs the boy.

He nods. "Okay, I'm Abhey. We should go to town hall."

Abhey leads us to a one story white building with pillars on both sides of the entrance. "This is the chief's office. He pretty much rules all of Scalia."

We then follow him to a big wooden door with the words 'Herbwell' on it with gold letters. Abhey knocks on the door knocker and we all wait. A man with a black suit opens the door. His hands are webbed and he has a long green tail below his back.

"What brings you children here?" the man asks.

"I'm Eoz Pawzord and this is my twin sister and our two friends. We are here to fight on your side of the war," I announce with confidence.

He looks at us, weighing if we are stong enough to fight. "Very well then, Abhey you may go. I need to talk to these children."

Without complaining Abhey obeys Chief Herbwell's commands and leaves the room.

"You don't seem like your Scalians or humanoids at all. Why do you want to fight in our army?" the chief questions.

Eilsel takes a step up. "We are human allies."

I try not to wince. I'd known we would have to lie if we wanted to fight at all.

"And how would I know that you aren't Auroran spies, may I ask?"

I speak before my brain agrees. "Give us training. Make us kill Aurorans if we have to. Please, just let us fight."

The chief considers for a moment before saying, "Fine. We have one week of training before we plan our first Attack. If you can out work everyone else I will let you on the troop."

We all thank him and begin to leave the room.

"Wait—don't go just yet. I'm only letting you do this because we are low on soldiers." He opens his mouth as if he were to say something else, but then closes it.

Abhey is waiting for us outside of the building, fiddling with his tail.

"Where do we go for training?" I ask him.

He jumps up, startled. "Oh! I didn't see you there. Umm, we have to be there tonight at 7 o'clock sharp."

"Okay, thank you."

When we arrive at the bootcamp some packs are lined up against a wooden bench. Abhey is standing over by some other teenagers.

He motions to us. "Come over here!"

While we walk over I can't help notice how few of us there are.

"Is this everyone?" I ask Abhey. "I hope not. There's hardly enough people for one troop."

After a few minutes, more people arrive. Everyone is a different age. There are people our age all the way to a few who are elderly.

"Okay everyone, my name is Jamison, but you will call me Chief. I am the leader of this army. We are passing out uniforms now and training will start at four o'clock tomorrow. There are 30 tents. 25 people per tent. Any extras will sleep outside."

"I doubt there will be any extras," Sciprus whispers.

"Yeah, if anything there will be too many tents," Wren adds.

Once we were all in our tents I couldn't help but worry what it will be like fighting in an army if I can't even shoot an arrow for the life of me. I know Eilsel will be a superstar at this and so will Wren. I've never actually seen Sciprus hunt so I don't have a clue about him.

A man with a gruff voice sets the alarm for three o'clock and says, "Lights out!"

In the morning... Well actually, it isn't really morning. Under any other circumstance I would still be asleep tucked in my bed at home. Anyway, we all put on our new camouflage uniforms and assemble in the main meeting area.

"All right, everyone. Today we're going to work on archery," Chief says.

All the trees have targets painted on them. "Group up in fours and go to a tree where you can begin to shoot your arrows at the targets. I will be walking around keeping tabs," Chief explains.

Wren, Eilsel, Sciprus and I choose a tree.

"Umm, guys? Sciprus and I don't have bows," I say once we are settled at the tree.

"I'll get some for us," Sciprus says.

"From where?" I ask.

But he has already left. Eilsel is already shooting her arrows at the target and making every single one.

"How do you do that?" I ask her.

"Shh! I'm trying to focus," she answers.

I look for some small stones on the ground and start chucking them at the tree flicking my risk.

"Well, well, Eoz. What are you doing?" I jump and almost squeal.

I'm so glad I didn't because the voice belongs to Chief Jamison.

"Oh me? I was waiting for Sciprus to come back with some extra bows," I say, nervously.

"Well, we don't have any," she replies. "You will have to use your sister's bow."

"Umm…" I say, as Eilsel walks over to see what all the fuss is about.

"Eoz is right. There is no way I'm gonna let her use my precious bow."

Jamison glares at her. "Don't make me regret accepting you to the troop?"

Eilsel sighs, but reluctantly hands me the bow and arrow.

"She isn't very good," Eilsel mutters under her breath.

I hold up the bow and slide the arrow between the wood and string. Pulling back on the arrow I take a breath hoping I won't humiliate myself in front of the chief. When I release, the arrow skids through the air and falls onto the grass in front of the tree instead of merely sticking to it. A loud sigh erupts from Chief Jamison.

"Eoz, come with me. You too, Sciprus," she says.

Prepared to be immediately kicked out, I walk glumly behind her.

"Eoz, what makes you think you can fight?" she asks once we are out of range of the target trees.

I look at Sciprus and then back at Agnes. "I just think I can. It feels right." I look down, not bearing to hear her response.

"And...?" she prompts.

"We need to win this war, for Fantasticals and Scalians alike." I explain.

Chief's mouth draws a straight line. "Fantasticals?

"Uhh... you know. They are the cause of the war," Sciprus chimes in.

"I guess you're right." Chief said.

Chief Jamison leads us to a white shed west from the campsite. "This is the weapons shed."

She goes inside and clatters around the small room. "You two stay here."

Scipris and I shrug, but obey her orders. A few other soldiers pass by on horseback holding javelins and shields. One has Scalian armor, but the other I don't recognize.

"Sciprus, what kind of armor is that?" I ask.

"Hmmm, it looks like Flare armor, but I'm not quite sure," Sciprus pauses. "Wait, what if he's not a Scalian, what if he's a Flare! We need to tell Chief."

We both stand up and run to the door of the shed.

"Chief Jamison, there's a Flare on our training ground!" I shout from outside the shed.

"There is? Where?"

"They are coming from the javelin arena," Sciprus adds.

"All right, I'm coming out, but then after a minute, the Chief says, "Hey kids, the door's stuck."

Sciprus looks at me. "Oh no, this is really bad."

I nod at Sciprus while trying to jiggle the door open. "We should go warn the others. Chief we'll be right back to get you out."

"Okay, good luck," she calls.

Sciprus and I run into the line of tents, hoping there will be a sign of the Flare. They aren't in the main area. However, I hear a faint scream coming from the trees near the Archers' Arena.

"Let's go," Sciprus says.

"We will be too late if we go by foot. Let's take the horses," I decide.

"I've never ridden a horse before," Sciprus announces.

I smile. "Well, there's a first time for everything."

On the north fence all the horses are tied up, some are tacked with saddles and bridals, but some aren't. I untie one of the tacked horses, and mount it.

"Get on Sciprus!"

"Oh, no way I'm getting on that," he says.

I glare at him. "Sciprus, our troop is at risk. Get on the horse."

He rolls his eyes. "Fine."

"Giddy up, Goliath!" I chant. I learned his name from his name tag on his bridal.

"I think I'm gonna be sick!" Sciprus yells from behind me.

"Don't worry we're almost there," I reply.

While we gallop through the trees I hear more screams and the clash of swords. I really hope that Eilsel and Wren are okay.

Once we get about ten yards from the Archers' Arena, we dismount Goliath. We sprint over through the trees.

"Eoz, Sciprus! over here!" Eilsel calls from behind a tree.

144

We run over to the tree where they are standing.

"There's a troop of Flares," Wren explains.

I look over at the clearing and at least twenty Flares in the arena.

"We need a plan," I say.

"Yeah, how did they even get here?" a familiar deep voice comes from beside me.

I turn around, "Abhey!"

He smiles. "Really though, we need a plan."

Suddenly, I think of something that might work.

"Okay Abhey, gather the rest of the swordsmen and bring them here. Wren and Sciprus, collect some of the archers and lead a diversion. Eilsel and I will round up everyone else and we'll try to fight the Flares off." I command my friends.

"Okay, let's go," Abhey says.

I see Wren and Sciprus running towards the horses. Their troop will ride away from the camp as far as possible with the soldiers following them. Hopefully, the distraction will give us time to prepare everyone else to face the Flares when they come back.

The Scalians are so busy shooting targets on the trees, they don't seem to notice the Flare soldiers trying to make their way through. One of the Flares dismounts her horse and walks up to a Scalian soldier. She says something to him, but I can't make out her words. The Scalian nods, and starts to run in the opposite direction. Another Scalian follows him, leaving his bow and arrow behind.

After a moment I hear an arrow shoot through the air right past my ear. I turn around, and it turns out it was a *Scalian* who attempted to shoot me. It's not long until I realize that a lot of these 'Scalian' soldiers aren't really Scalian.

A lot of them are Flares.

"Eoz, we have imposters among us," Eilsel says timidly.

I nod. "Follow me."

Eilsel grips her squeezes her bow and follows me.

"Hey, grab your bows we're going to fight!" Eilsel shouts at a crowd of soldiers.

They all obey her and march into the clearing. Thankfully, Wren and Sciprus' diversion is working—there seem to be a lot less Flares than there were earlier. I have a strong feeling that Wren used her Mage powers. Scalians hide on the edge of the clearing, inching away from the enemy.

"Line up!" I scream to the soldiers.

I don't think they'll listen, but I've seen Jamison give that command when we practice our squad training. However, surprisingly enough everyone lines up into a platoon and waits for me to give the signal to fire their weapons.

"Fire!" I command after a moment.

The troop fires their arrows at the few Flare soldiers. It's the first time I've ever seen war, and let me tell you now, it's not pretty. Blood goes everywhere. Soldiers are knocked to the ground, and people are killed in front of my very own eyes. I'm not sure how I imagined war, but the reality is nothing like I thought it would be.

Soon enough, all the Flares we can see lay dead, and silence settles. Only nine Scalians are injured. After the battle, everyone goes back to camp for supper and oddly, it's like nothing happened at all.

However, after someone realizes that Jamison is still missing, the five of us—Wren, Sciprus, Abhey, Eilsel and I run back to the shed—and eventually set her free. Let's just say it involves Sciprus, a war axe and a blanket, but we won't get into details.

"Where are you going?" Eilsel asks one night after supper.

"Nowhere." Wren and I giggle and scurry back to our tents and change out of our uniforms.

"Let's go to the river," I whisper, as we run outside of camp.

"I dare you to dive in!" I exclaim.

"No way. It's freezing," Wren replies.

We sit on a patch of grass in the starry night.

"I have some nuts from supper. Do you want any?" I ask.

Wren nods, so I split them up and hand half of them over.

"You know, long after we are grown up and have families or something, we are going to still be friends," Wren says.

I think about her words. "I agree. It feels like we have known each other for years, even though it's only been two weeks."

"Yeah. Hey Eoz, do you want to stay here tonight?" Wren asks me.

"Yeah, that would be nice."

Just before dawn, Wren and I make it back to the trading camp.

"Where'd you guys go?" Eilsel asks in a sleepy voice.

"Just down to the creek," Wren replies.

I tuck my hair behind my ears. Eilsel frowns and walks away.

"Eilsel, wait up!" I call.

"What do you want, Eoz?" Eilsel turns around to look at me.

"What's your deal? Are you mad or something?" I ask.

"I'm not mad. I just don't get why you didn't tell me that you were going to the river with Wren."

"It's a creek, not a river," I reply.

Eilsel rolls her eyes. "Look, I don't really care. But if we are going to be in this war together, we need to stick together."

COUNTDOWN

EILSEL PAWZORD

Training for war is mind-dimming, which right now is a good thing. Ever since Eoz told Ruben we were here to fight in the war, my body has been here and my mind elsewhere. I'm only twelve; I don't want to kill people! Yet Eoz, Wren, and even Sciprus have seemed fine with the idea and still do. I don't understand! Why didn't Eoz tell me she wanted to fight in the war?

I think back to what seems like years in the past, which was actually only a week or two ago, when I shot kids with paint for PE. It was fun and it didn't really hurt them, but now I wonder if war is like that.

Is it *fun* to wound or kill *live beings* for people? Am I cruel to have gone through with the PE game and shot people with that paint and enjoyed it?

I don't want to have to think about it. I don't want to have to have these thoughts running around my head, telling me that maybe Eoz likes war, that she wants to hurt people. I know she doesn't, as she thought I was slightly mean for hunting the animals back in Peril Forest. Now that I think about it, is war the same as hunting? I know I hurt the animals when I shoot them, but I always tried to make it quick so they didn't have to suffer.

I can't do this. I don't want to fight in this war, and I can't fight in this war. Maybe Eoz can, but not me. I came on this journey not to hurt, but to help. I want to help the Aurorans, the Flares, the Scalians, the Prowls, us and any other Fantastical that are still out there—everyone really. There has to be a peaceful solution, right?

I understand that we're supposed to be doing this for a cause. We don't want the Aurorans to take over the world and exterminate the humanoid species, but if we exterminate *them* in battles doesn't that make us just as bad? And I know not all Aurorans or Flares are horrible people. There's the kids from school—well, not Jeremy, duh—and Red, the funny boy in the Flare army. Even his brother, Agni, didn't seem all bad.

Sciprus's voice snaps me out of my thoughts. "Eilsel, are you paying attention? They're about to announce who the commanders are, and then those commanders will choose their troops."

The officials rattle off names for Frog, Snake, Gator, and Lizard platoons. I breathe a sigh of relief when my name isn't called.

"We have decided to add in one more platoon... Eoz Pawzord will be the commander of Griffin Squadron," Chief Agnes shouts.

The whole army goes silent, and I know what they're thinking. *A kid? A kid is going to lead us into battle?* I know Eoz will be deadly proficient at this job based upon when she made a plan for us to sneak through the camp by the border. In fact, she may even be too proficient. But last time there were gaps in her plan, nothing big enough for me to worry about but still they existed. Hopefully, she wouldn't miss important details when we went into battle. *Battle?* What am I thinking?

Just because Eoz is a commander doesn't mean I can automatically agree to fight in her battalion. I know she'll ask me, and I know no matter what I say she'll still go to war.

I guess I'm okay with other people fighting, but I can't do it myself. Does that make me a coward? I don't know if it does, and it's not that I'm scared of dying, or getting injured. I'm scared of what I could do to the other side. Maybe there's some way I could help the Scalians without hurting anyone? I know I can't—I won't, rather— hurt anyone. But what if I have to hurt someone?

I won't let Eoz go into battle alone, no matter how many things about this goes against my moral code. And so I am the first one to cheer for Eoz, and then Wren, then Sciprus. Ruben and Abhey start to clap, and the rest of the army soon follows suit. Eoz looks at me gratefully, and even though my head is screaming at me not to, I smile back.

* * *

I retreat to my tent. Half is mine, half is Sciprus's, but he's the only one who uses it. I've gotten so used to sleeping outside that I just roll out a sleeping bag and that's that. It's nearly the full moon again, and I swear I can smell rain in the air. It must be a wolf thing.

Actually, about that... It kind of bothers me that I don't know what type of wolf I am. Last time I checked, wolves aren't mythical creatures. I know I'm a Fantastical, not a Prowl, because when I think about Fantasticals it just feels *right* in a way that Prowls don't. The Ninth Faction, that's Eoz and I.

Ugh, who am I kidding. This is a topic I almost never think about, since it isn't a pressing issue. But I don't want to have to think about the war right now, so I wonder about my power instead. Even Aikai couldn't tell what type of wolf I am. So far, all the things I can do are exactly what any wolf could do. I sigh. I don't need to resolve this right now, but what I do need to do is stop this feeling that keeps eating at me.

Before I have time to think about it, Eoz walks up behind me. I pretend to be busy by looking at the setting sun and the rising moon. Eoz sits down, a commander's badge adorned with a griffin on her shirt, which will soon be replaced with armor.

"So," I start. "Nice job on getting to be a commander."

"Thanks!" Eoz says, smiling.

I can tell that Eoz has no idea I feel so strongly about war, and if that's bad or good I still don't know.

"So, do you want to be one of my soldiers?" Eoz asks casually.

I know I should say yes, just like I told myself I would when Eoz became a commander. But deep down, I don't want to. Even though it's my sister/best friend asking, even though I love our cause, I won't kill people for it.

But my mind flips back to 'Help her, Eilsel!' and then I'm at war not with the Auroran-Flares, but with myself. On the one hand, I want to help my sister win the battle. I want to stop people on my side from dying. But on the other hand, I know that can't—won't, I know I can—take a life, even if it was to save someone on our side.

"I'm not sure I can do that, Eoz," I mumble.

She looks at me, the expression on her face totally and utterly shocked. "Wh-what do you mean? If you're worried about me, I'll keep myself safe. You too, plus Sciprus and Wren of course. Just trust me, okay?"

"I trust you, Eoz. And I am absolutely worried about you, but I also know you can take care of yourself," I say quietly.

Just as I'm about to continue, Eoz cheers, "So you'll do it?"

When I don't answer right away, Eoz leaps into a half-angry, half-annoyed speech, her point being "You're a hunter! You hunt stuff! This is no different."

Eoz is right a lot of the time, but this time I know she isn't. To Eoz's (and my own) surprise, I retort, "I hunt *animals* in *forests*, not *people* in *war-zones*. I killed the animals because we had to eat, Eoz, not because I got mad at them! People are different! They have more complex thoughts and feelings, and they have friends and family. I can't just take all that away from them for this war that—that is my fault!"

"By that logic, it's my fault as well, Eilsel," my sister says coldly.

"Listen, Eoz. Remember how the headmaster said they knew we were Fantasticals and that they could give us a head start, but that they'd need to report us to the Auroran-Flare army? If I hadn't said we should try to get expelled instead of just leaving, the army might have just forgotten about us. Maybe they would've decided that we never actually existed, and that it was some sort of hoax. We could've warned the Scalians, and then hidden with Aikai until this all passed over. Maybe all the factions excluding the Fantasticals could've made some sort of peace agreement. We were the final thing that made both sides decide to go to war! And it was *my fault*," I finish.

Eoz looks as though she can't decide whether to argue with me further or tell me it's not actually my fault.

Unfortunately, she goes with the first option. "But Eilsel—"

"It's against all my morals, Eoz. I really can't do this," I interject.

I hate to let her down, and as I'm about to apologize when Eoz deals a sickening verbal blow.

"You're such a coward, Eilsel. All these people are out here sacrificing themselves, and you say you won't even fight. Well, I'm not like you. I will help them, while you won't. Sometimes I wonder how *you're* supposed to be my twin. Maybe Aikai lied and you're actually just some Fantastical or even a Prowl and not my sister."

I almost want to cry, but instead I fight her words with my own. "Well, who are you? Where is the sister I used to know? You're some blood-thirsty monster, not because you're a Fantastical, but because you're willing to go through with this war. You say you're risking your life, and you are, but you're going to kill a bunch of people who are just following orders just because!"

Eoz recoils, looking hurt, then snaps back, "You're so childish!"

I reply angrily with, "You're too mature!"

"I am not!" Eoz shouts.

"Well, apparently you're too old for me, and you need to go and hang out with your new friend who is so much better than I ever was!" I say bitterly.

Eoz looks guilty for a moment before retorting, "Maybe I don't want to spend time with a coward like you! Maybe that's a good thing, as I'm a commander and you're not!"

Eoz doesn't know half of it. I could *never* be a commander. It would *not* work. At all. While I think of this, I don't speak, and now Eoz probably thinks that I'm jealous of her. I sigh. I was stupid to bring this up.

Eoz shoves her battle plans in my face, and I pale instantly. These plans are really good, but there is one fatal flaw. They're incredibly well thought out, but there is one issue. The plans don't show how many soldiers the Auroran-Flares have. I know that we have at least ninety-nine troops in the Griffin Squadron and that I would be the hundredth member, yet I don't know about the other platoons. The issue with this is that there could be hundreds more of the combined Auroran-Flare army, and we wouldn't even know! We'd be totally outnumbered and would lose in minutes. But maybe Eoz *does* know how many soldiers the other side has, and she just forgot to write it down.

I ask, "How many troops does the enemy have?"

To my dismay, my sister only shrugs.

"Ruben was supposed to be collecting data, but he was caught before he was able to get it. We have little time, so our only option is to move forward," she explains.

"But, we don't have enough information, Eoz! We could lose because of this one tiny detail!" I shout.

Surprise flashes across the newly commissioned commander's face. Crickets chirp in the background. Even though I've been arguing with Eoz, I haven't yelled yet. I don't shout angrily very often, so I can understand why 'Commander Pawzord' as she's called now would be so astonished.

"You're jealous, aren't you? *You* wanted to be the commander, didn't you? Well, the authorities chose me, Eilsel, not you. Just because you were the hunter back before all this doesn't make me incompetent! I can do this, Eilsel! The plans will get us through this, don't you see?" she shouts back.

"I am *not* jealous! In fact, I was basically praying that I wouldn't be a commander! I've never wanted to hurt people, and I don't really get how you've never seen that!" I admit.

Eoz looks at me with a face full of regret. I know she didn't mean the majority of the things she said earlier, and neither do I.

"Eilsel, come with me. I will prove to you that I can do this, but I want—no, I need—you by my side if this is going to work. So, are you with me?"

"Eoz... I'll come with you. I will make no promise to fight, but I will go with you to the battlefield." I promise.

"That is all I ask." Eoz says solemnly.

She gets up and leaves the tent. The moon has risen to its peak now, and the stars twinkle in the night sky, oblivious to the rising tension below. The moon is quite bright, as it is nearly full. I know what I have to do, and I will be defying all orders to do it. But if my sister, friends, and all the Scalians are to survive this, it must be done.

A single drop of rain falls on my head. It can only represent the coming storm that will make—or break—us all.

COMMANDER

EOZ PAWZORD

"**M**arch!" I scream so even the soldiers in the very back can hear my piercing shriek.

Two-by-two we march on our horses into the colorless night. Sword in hand I lead my troop to the battlefield. The air has smelled like mud and we all smell like socks because there wasn't a lake at our old campground. Although there happened to be mud—lots and lots of mud.

"How much longer?" Eilsel complains.

I roll my eyes. "We won't be there for another hour."

Eilsel lowers her head but stays quiet for the rest of the way.

COMMANDER

As the clearing in the woods came into view, Eilsel ran ahead of everyone to be the first to set up her tent. The soldiers took their small tents out of their bags and put them up in an orderly manner. It isn't long until all fifty tents are set up in a circle along the tree line. My tent is in the very center of the clearing. I've paired up with Wren because everyone needed a partner to share a tent with. Eilsel has been in a tent with Sciprus, only because I refused to stay with her if she won't fight in the army.

"Commander, may I speak with you?" a voice calls from the outside of the tent.

I unzip it and climb out. "Yes, Abhey."

"We should leave for the battle at five o'clock tomorrow. The snow has been very heavy, so the horses need to be well fed tonight."

"Okay, please tell Section Four to start feeding the horses," I command him.

"Very well." Abhey says before leaving me alone in the dark.

"Wren. Wren, are you awake?"

There isn't an answer. I lay back on my side, but I can't fall asleep. I turn on the lantern, and it sheds a warm glow onto the canvas of the tent.

"Wren!" I repeat in a louder voice.

A minute passes. Nothing. A few minutes more go by. Still nothing. I check my watch—it's only one o'clock. I undo the leather strap on my watch and hold it so it's just hovering over her ear. The tic, tic, tic sound is sure to annoy her even if she was asleep.

It doesn't take very long until she sits up rubbing her eyes. "Eoz, what are you doing?"

"Sorry, but I couldn't sleep," I confess softly.

"Oh, umm… what's the matter?" she asks.

I sigh. "Well, I suppose I'm just scared for the battle. What Eilsel said was right. We could be outnumbered by hundreds or even thousands of men."

"And women," she adds.

I nod and Wren yawns. I feel badly for waking her but I need to talk to someone.

"I just don't think I'm ready." My voice trembles and before long I'm sobbing into Wren's lap.

It's still dark when I wake up. The bitter air bites our noses as we change back into our armor and saddle up the horses. My watch reads four o'clock, which gives us one hour to prepare. Everyone is rolling up their tents, feeding the horses and sharpening swords.

"Eilsel, c'mon get your arrow we're leaving soon."

"For the last time Eoz, I'm not fighting as a soldier."

"Uh huh. Well, if you're not going to fight as a soldier you aren't going to fight in my troop," I quip.

Eilsel looks at me astonished. "Fine."

Everyone is on their horses ready to go. I lead my horse Goliath to the front of the crowd. As I mount my horse I clear my throat before we go.

"All right, everyone," I announce. "Congratulations on making it here today. I want to say that we are all fighting for our freedom, for the Fantasticals freedom. Today is just the beginning. We shall fight not for ourselves but for the entire world."

Everyone cheers and raises their weapons. With that, we ride out into the distance.

Looking at our enemies I can already tell we are outnumbered. Not only that, they have canons and angry horses.

"Here we are," I say to Wren.

"Fire!" The commander screams from the Aurorans. Arrows shoot from their side.

"Shields up!" I cry.

My silver shield reflects the morning light from the sun. Everyone knows exactly what to do. A section of the soldiers gallop forward firing arrows off their bows. It isn't long before the battle is in full swing. Cannons fire, taking out some of our men. Paramedics rush to them taking them to tents.

"Gallop, Goliath!" I chant and give him a tight squeeze.

The horse gallops into the Auroran army. Someone tries to shoot an arrow at me but it deflects off my shield and onto her horse. Another canon fires. "Poof!" The canon blows up snow rolling down the mountain side.

"Avalanche!" someone calls.

Everyone on horseback rides off away from the mountains. A few more soldiers are killed. I scan the horizon for Eilsel. I can't see her anywhere. *What if she isn't okay?*

An Auroran soldier rides up beside me.

"You shall not win this," he yells, holding his sword up to me.

I grip my sword even harder and slash it at his waist.

"Winning won't be that easy," he says as he deflects my attack with his sword.

I fight him until he loses his balance and slows down. I ride even faster, leaving him behind. It isn't long until Wren catches up to me.

"Have you seen Eilsel and Sciprus?" Wren shouts.

"No, I haven't seen Sciprus anywhere."

Wren gives me a look. "And what about Eilsel?"

I sigh. "I don't know."

"Eoz, you should know where she is. Didn't you send her somewhere?" Wren inquires.

I shake my head. "Maybe she's with Sciprus."

Now Wren looks furious. "Eoz!"

There are a lot less soldiers now than there were at the start of the battle. There are many injured soldiers being carried by someone else on a horse. There are even more that are practically dying of thirst. But we don't have a choice, we have to keep on going.

Once the mountains are out of view everyone dismounts their horses and we fight with our good old swords and bows. It didn't occur to me how nasty wars really are. No wonder Eilsel didn't want any part of this situation.

But now, I know I don't have a choice. I have to fight. The battle goes on and more and more people die from each side. I can hear the clanging of swords and the shooting of arrows from afar. The stained crystal white snow is creating bloody splotches across the battlefield. I know Eilsel and I are supposed to be in our own private war, one that wouldn't have existed if it hadn't been for this larger war. Now, fighting for my life, I can't help but wonder where Eilsel is and if she's safe.

RED AND BLUE

EILSEL PAWZORD

I run past ferns and icky pond-water, panting heavily. I had to leave David, my horse, at the battlefield. He wouldn't be able to fit through some of the nooks and crannies that I'm using to save time.

Ever since I realized that Eoz didn't have all the information she needed to craft a good plan, I've been plotting my escape. I'm not deserting the army, I'm going to collect the missing data.

To keep my mind off my worries while I jog, I try to figure out what my job title is. I'm not a soldier, that much is clear. I'm not fighting things, I'm gathering information. Yet, I'm not exactly scouting ahead, and I'm not a true spy. I've gone through none of the training to become one.

A familiar voice snaps me out of my thoughts. "Eilsel, what are you doing?!"

I whirl around to see Wren on top of David. So he *can* fit through those cracks... I wish I knew that when I first started running.

"It's not what you think. I'm not abandoning you guys or anything, so don't worry," I say.

"You sure look like you are, but I'll listen to what you have to say," she says, her green eyes flickering.

"When I saw Eoz's plans, one thing stuck out to me. We don't know how many soldiers the opposing side has, and that could kill us all. I'm going to sneak into the Auroran-Flare's commanding officer's tent and break into their records. I'm pretty sure they'll have them, and then I'll bring them back to Eoz so she can reconstruct her plan to better our chances of victory and survival. Also... this way I don't have to fight," I explain.

I falter slightly at the end, but I don't think Wren notices.

"Right. You're going to get yourself murdered if you go in there with no backup. So, even though this is a stupid idea, I'm coming with you. But I will never forgive you if something happens to Sciprus or Eoz and I can't help because I'm here, you got that?"

I nod frantically. I could definitely use the help.

"Hop on," she says.

I walk over to David and use the stirrups to climb up behind Wren. Without a moment's notice, the horse takes off running. David is a smaller horse, but boy can he run fast. Soon I'm visibly struggling to hold on, but that's not much of a problem because before long we come across the enemy camp.

"Huh," I whisper. "They must have moved, because last time I checked their camp was a lot farther away from here."

Wren shows she agrees with a thumbs up, yet stays quiet. Being too loud could get us both killed, captured, or worse.

"Okay, there isn't much cover. I'll have to get really, and I mean *really* lucky if I'm going to be able to sneak in there," I say worriedly.

"I can help you with that," Wren whispers.

I turn to look at her. "I thought your powers couldn't fool that many people. What changed? Also, would the illusion affect me? 'Cause it would be pretty weird if I couldn't see myself."

"One, I practiced. Two, no, it wouldn't. Come on, the sooner we get back with this info the better," Wren answers.

She scrunches her eyes up and then opens them. A look of intense concentration crosses her face, and then she walks out into the open. I follow her. There are barely any people here, and most of the ones that are seem to be either sick or wounded. They don't show signs of seeing us when we pass, so I can only assume that Wren's magic is working.

"Okay, just walk in there. I'll stand guard out here," Wren tells me quietly.

I nod. Even though we're invisible to the eye, we're definitely not invisible to the ear, so I tiptoe to the biggest tent in the area. It's reddish orangish, a different color from the other light blue ones. I open the flap after checking to make sure no one's looking. It would be pretty weird if it just *opened* with no one nearby, and it's not very breezy. Actually, scratch that. The wind seems to be picking up, but I still can't risk it.

The inside of the tent is split in two halves. On the left it's the neatest thing ever, even more than how Eoz's part of our room used to look. The right looks like a disaster zone, with clothes and armor scattered everywhere. Without warning, the flap opens again and I leap for cover even though I'm invisible.

It's the soldier and commander we saw at the very beginning of our journey! Their names are Agni and Red, if I remember correctly.

"Agniiiiii, why can't we go to the battle?" Red whines.

"I told you, you're too young. Also, General Hawken will be here to see us shortly," Agni explains, clearly exasperated.

"Hawken's coming?" Agni says, eyes wide, and then immediately starts running around chanting joyfully, "Hawken's coming, Hawken's coming!"

I almost smile and then realize that Red and I would be great friends if we weren't on two different sides of this war, and that if Red was at the battlefield Eoz would be trying to kill him and he her.

I'm hiding behind what must be Agni's sleeping bag, and flinch away when he sits down on it. I back up slowly, and look around for something that seems official. I do see something, but it's not at all where I expected. Agni is reading a piece of parchment, and I can see a battle plan on it.

This is going to be incredibly difficult. I can't just wait for him to put it down, as that would take too long, so what should I do? Just then, the stupidest plan ever crosses through my mind. No one really knows what the two Fantasticals look like, right? And there's all that armor scattered on the floor... I'm sure they won't miss it.

Whenever Agni and Red aren't looking, I grab a piece of armor and strap it on over my tunic. I then go outside the tent and ask Wren to remove the illusion spell.

"Are you sure? This is the stupidest thing I've ever heard, even more so than punching Jeremy," she whispers.

I give Wren a wayward grin.

"I'll be fine," I say curtly. "You trust me, right?"

Wren nods and waves her hand. She gestures for me to go back in the tent, and I do. She's still invisible to the soldiers, so she continues to wait outside.

I push open the tent flag and inwardly cringe as the commander and soldier turn to look at me.

"You knock before entering, soldier," Agni says.

I nod, even though it's a tent and honestly how could I knock? Red bursts out laughing. Agni shoots me some sort of 'what did you just say' look. Aw, shoot. I must've said that out loud.

"Sorry, Commander, sir," I apologize.

"I don't think I've seen you around. No one else here is my age and you seem to be. That's so cool! What's your name?" Red asks energetically.

I try to think fast. I really shouldn't tell him my real name. That would be stupid of me. Gah, I'm taking too long! I end up just blurting out the first thing I think of.

"Blue! I'm Blue," I say.

"Ooh, nice name! I'm Red Flare, and this is my older brother, Agni. He's the commander and all, but he's actually a big softie!" Red proclaims.

Agni looks like he's about to strangle his younger brother, but instead he speaks. "Why are you here, soldier? I would assume you'd be too young to fight, but still. How did you even get into this platoon? The only reason Red is here is because... never mind."

When I don't immediately answer, he commands, "Answer, soldier!"

This time, I have an answer. "I'm uhh, proficient with a bow, sir."

It isn't technically a lie. I am good with a bow, and it did get me into an army, just not this one.

I know I'm running short on time. At this rate I might just grab the papers and run, even though it would be quite stupid. Whelp, I have no other option. In one fell swoop I swipe the plans from Agni and run out the door.

"After that soldier!" Agni yells, but none of the soldiers here are strong enough to even stand up.

They do, however, look at their commander apologetically. Red shoots out of the tent and starts chasing after me, so I pick up the pace.

"We gotta go!" I shout, uncaring that everyone can hear me.

Wren looks at me in horror. I really don't know what I'm doing, but I keep running. Soon I can't see the campsite, but I can't see Wren either. Unfortunately, I know why she was scared for me now. She must've known that I was running straight into a dead end, with stone cliffs around me that I can't possibly hope to climb.

I look around frantically for a way out, but all I notice is the weather. Clouds that had previously been few and far between are now many, and it starts to rain harder and harder with each passing minute. The sun is covered, and it gets dark. A chill runs down my spine and I shiver. All of this reminds me of one thing, one thing that I have always tried not to think about: the Demon-Bear.

It's ironic the way that no matter how hard I try to avoid it, the Demon-Bear always comes up in some way, shape, or form. But Red is not a Demon-Bear from out of my nightmares; he's a funny kid in an opposing army. I've even told Eoz that if there weren't a war going on, we could've been good friends.

Why does the Demon-Bear keep coming up, in my mind or in reality?

I turn my back to the wall and face the way I came in. Red walks through slowly, sword drawn.

"Uh, Blue, Agni told me this isn't a game. He says you're an enemy soldier for the Scalians, but you don't exactly look like a Scalian. What's going on?" he asks, his voice quivering.

I can't see a point in arguing, but I do have to make him believe that I'm just a normal human. It would be seriously bad if he were to catch on that I'm not what I seem.

"I am with the Scalians. And yeah, I'm just a human. My sister is out there fighting for her life, and so are some of my friends. They're fighting against your side because we don't believe it's right to take what's not yours. I'm not there, so I am not a soldier. I don't think I ever will be," I state.

I might have gone a bit overboard there. I don't need Red to understand that I won't fight him even though I do indeed have a weapon on me.

"Why not?"

Aww, shoot. There goes that.

"I don't like fighting... I don't like killing," I say honestly.

"But *why*?" Red continues.

I think for a moment. I know that I don't want to kill anyone. I've always been like that. Have I ever really sat down and asked myself, in a brutally honest manner, why?

"I've always wanted to help people, not injure them," I answer.

"Me too... but are you sure that's all?" he prompts.

Here we go again. I need to get out of here, and I'm standing around talking to the enemy. Eventually, his older brother will get here, and when that happens I'll be dead meat. In the end, I'm just trying to get away from the other answer. I just thought of it, yet I already know it to be true.

If I try to kill someone, no matter the cause, I will be just like the Demon-Bear. I could scar someone exactly the same way the beast did to me. Someone else could be afraid, someone else would feel how I feel... but I don't want that. I think I've finally come to a separate conclusion that relates entirely to this one.

The reason I'm scared of the Demon-Bear is because I don't want to be like it was. The creature was a malevolent beast, and it attacked from the shadows unpredictably. I don't know why it did what it did. Was that just its nature, or did someone make it that way?

I will most likely never know. But if the later of the two really is what happened... it could just as easily happen to me. And so, I give Red my real answer.

"There is someone that I don't want to be like. That I never want to be like. It was violent for as far as I know no reason, and I don't want to act as it did."

"I can understand that. I don't really like fighting, either. And... I feel a bit bad about this, but Agni's always talking about war and I don't agree with him, like at all," Red says.

I feel slightly better about not agreeing with Eoz and disliking fighting.

"Yeah. My sister seems to be all about fighting too. She's always like, 'Ei-'" I cut myself off mid sentence. I nearly exposed my real name, and that would be bad. And then, one second later, there goes that.

"Blue's not your real name, is it? Who really are you?" Red asks, with what I think might be a rare moment of insight.

"You really think I'd tell you that? You're technically the enemy," I say coldly.

Red looks at me. "I don't want to be your enemy."

"Huh. I don't want to be your enemy, either. Just call me Blue, okay?" I say, avoiding Red's actual question.

"In that case, I'm Red. Not sir, or whatever you were calling me before." He grins. "I'll see you again, Blue. I've never met someone else who doesn't like fighting, so now... Agni! I think I lost her!" Red walks away without another word.

I sneak back to Wren, and we hop on David, racing to the battlefield as fast as possible. I can hear thunder, and lightning strikes somewhere in the distance. I tuck the plans safely in my satchel, where they can't get even more wet. Thankfully, they're not too damaged and you can still read them.

I think about all that's happened today. I do think that I'll see Red again, and when I do I'll have to thank him. He helped me come to the conclusion that I shouldn't feel bad about not being a soldier. And maybe I helped him, too.

THE NON-EXISTANT FAVOR

EILSEL PAWZORD

"Eilsel, why in the nine factions are you wearing Auroran armor?" Eoz asks. Her face is stained with a red colored substance that I really hope is mud and not blood. "Also, where have you *been*? We fought off the first wave of Auroran-Flares, but we have reason to believe there may be more on the way." Eoz gulps at the end of this sentence, but remains determined as always.

"Here," I say. "This will answer your questions."

I shove the battleplans I stole from Agni and Red into her hands.

"Where did you even get these?" she wonders. "Oh, never mind. But these look like Auroran-Flare battleplans... they have so many more soldiers than us. We've lost so many lives already. It's going to be almost impossible to win," my twin frets.

And she's right, the odds do *not* look good for us. Eoz turns to look up at me from where she's standing on the battlefield. I dismount David, and Wren takes him to go look for Sciprus.

"Eilsel, we need you. You won't even have to kill people. I've found paint-arrows in our supplies, and I have absolutely no idea how they got there, but just use them on the Auroran-Flare's eyes. Our troops can then disarm them. I know you don't like war, and I think I understand why now. But Eilsel, I need your help."

"Fine. As long as it doesn't hurt the opposing side. But I am *not* a soldier, you got that?" I make sure my twin sister knows that I still refuse to be called a soldier. '

Eoz nods.

"Now, do you happen to have any blue paint-arrows?" I ask mischievously.

"Sure do!" Eoz grins, and for a moment it almost feels like we're back in Peril Forest, away from the war.

It's too bad that reality awaits us.

"Commander, enemy troops are marching this way," Abhey reports.

Eoz frowns. "Tell the archers to go up on that ridge. Eilsel, you're in charge of them. Now, soldiers, gather up!"

Before I run for the ridge with the other archers, I listen to Eoz rally the soldiers.

"The only way we're going to win is if we take them by surprise," Eoz shouts. "You need to disarm the winter-fire soldiers on the frontlines, then the archers will hit the others with paint-arrows in the eyes. Once they've done that, you'll disarm them. Only wound if necessary. Now, be ready, you're fighting for our freedom!"

Her words have definitely worked. Even from up on this ridge, I can see the soldiers cheering. The archers have all turned expectantly towards me. Oh. They think I'm going to give them orders just like Eoz.

"Uhh... right. We have a lot of paint arrows right here. We're going to shoot the enemy in the eyes with them, and then our ground soldiers will disarm them. Good luck guys, you got this!" I encourage the archers.

They seem unused to such a casual approach, but they knock their paint-arrows anyway. I do the same, and soon enough the enemy charges. Eoz's ground soldiers rush to meet them. Battle cries and the clashing of swords can be heard from below, and once our side manages to take care of those on the front line we'll shoot.

I can tell it's a hard battle. Eoz's troops are heavily outnumbered, and the other platoons won't be able to provide backup for a while. We're on our own. I watch Eoz. She is much better with a sword then she ever was with a bow, and one day she might even be some sort of master. The enemies she meets always seem to underestimate her despite the amount of soldiers she's already disarmed. She slips through their defenses and uses her sword to make theirs crash to the ground. Eoz is pretty good on the battlefield.

I turn to Sciprus. He's not nearly as good as Eoz, but his larger stature is proving to be incredibly useful. Since the majority of the Winter-Fires, as Eoz calls them, are adults, it helps that Sciprus is able to almost look eye to eye with some of the shorter ones. Sciprus uses his shield much more often than his sword, using it to repel his opponents' attacks. He then takes his sword out and uses it similarly to Eoz, but relies more on his strength than the element of surprise.

Wren seems to be using her Mage powers to confuse the troops she fights before disarming them. She can't fool all of them at once, she's too exhausted from disguising herself and I earlier, but she seems to be doing well just taking one at a time. The soldier she's currently attacking looks curiously at something I can't see, and then Wren kicks her in the stomach. I flinch. I know the soldier will be fine, and that it will just bruise, but I still don't like it. The soldier is shoved to the ground and Wren picks up her weapon.

Next I check on Abhey. He's fighting dirty, kicking snow at some of the Auroran-Flares' eyes. It's necessary, however, as Abhey is almost the opposite of Sciprus. He's a lot smaller, and not nearly as strong, but his creative maneuvers are keeping him alive. I can see his pale blue-grey eyes sparkle with determination all the way from over here. His normally blond hair is stained with mud and sweat, but thankfully not blood.

Ruben isn't doing so well. The area above one of his large amber eyes is scratched, and blood is trickling into it. I assume he's having a hard time seeing out of that eye. He's using a spear instead of a sword, which means he doesn't have to be as close to his opponents as those wielding swords. Just as one of the Winter-Fires is about to seriously injure him, another one of the soldiers hits the Auroran-Flare with her tail.

Finally, *finally* the front line is clear. I wave my hand at the army, which is our signal for 'get back, or else you'll be splattered with pink paint!' I pull my bowstring back and fire at the closest enemy. His eyes are splattered with bright green paint, and my sister rushes over to him and takes his sword and shield.

All around me, archers are attacking with paint. The battlefield is turned colorful, and the snow is now stained with paint as well as blood. Our army has still lost so many lives, but it looks like their sacrifice won't be in vain. Our surprise attack is working, and we're able to take the enemy soldiers down one by one.

Soon enough, the Auroran-Flares retreat. We've captured the vast majority of their forces, and the rest are tired and beaten. I smile. The Battle of Colorful Snow, as I've dubbed it, has been won!

The Archers and I climb down from the ridge we've been shooting from. The ground soldiers cheer, and so do we. After all this training, all this fighting, we've reached victory. And I didn't have to harm a single person to do so. Even that alone would make me proud.

"Eoz, we did it!" I shout.

Eoz takes one look at me and points her sword in my direction.

"Put the bow down, Winter-Fire," she growls.

I look at her, surprised. Then I realize what must've happened. The visor I had borrowed from Red had fallen over my face, so she can't see that it's me. I tear off the helmet and fling it on the ground.

"Uhh, sword away, please?" I ask.

Eoz laughs. "Sorry, Eilsel. I totally forgot you had on that armor. Maybe you should take it off, it's not fooling only me."

My twin is right, some of the Scalian troops are looking at me with distrust in their eyes. I pull the armor off, revealing the Scalian uniform tunic underneath. The Scalians sigh in relief.

We start walking back towards our horses. I can see David eating grass next to Eoz's horse, Goliath. The two are complete opposites in comparison. Goliath towers above David's head, yet the two seem to be at least tolerant of each other. Ehh, they probably got it from Eoz and I, the duo were practically at the other's throat when we first rode them. (Which was certainly an adventure, by the way.)

Sciprus and Wren are talking happily, and Sciprus seems to be about to get something off his chest, metaphorically speaking. I think he's about to tell her he really likes her, and I want to scream 'Do it, do it!' at him but I won't let the moment be ruined.

Just then, an arrow whizzes through the air straight towards Wren. Everything seems to slow down, and Eoz and I will never make it over there in time. Sciprus is there, though. What he does next I know will show up in my nightmares for many years to come.

He leaps in front of Wren, taking the arrow for her. It lodges right near his heart, and he falls to the ground. Time speeds up again, and suddenly my twin sister and I are right next to Sciprus and Wren, who is holding back tears.

"Medic! Get a medic over here!" I scream.

Sciprus is still alive. I know he can make it—he's strong.

"Wren..." he chokes out. "I need to tell you something. I-I've liked for a while now, and I've been t-trying to work up the n-nerve to tell you. You're s-smart, pretty and one of the b-best people I know. Wren... I love you."

Sciprus works up the last bit of his strength to sit up and kiss Wren on the cheek. He then slumps to the ground and goes limp.

Wren bursts out crying, despite having said many times that she never cries. Eoz looks like she wants to as well, but needs to be strong. As for me, I'm just sitting here, shocked. I don't want to move, and yet I do. I lean over to check his pulse. There is nothing.

Sciprus is dead.

FUTURE HISTORY

EOZ PAWZORD

After the battle I lead the remaining soldiers back to the training camp. Of course we are glad we won the battle, but an aching feeling remains in our stomachs due to the amount of lives we lost.

Especially Sciprus.

However, we try to make the best of things. We hold a small party at the camp to celebrate, but it's not as lively as we hoped. Fortunately I still have *most* of my friends left.

Eilsel is with some other youth archers hanging around the archery trees. She has her bow and arrow in hand and a big cheesy smile on her face. I'm honestly not sure where the smile came from, though.

"Hey!" I call.

Eilsel looks up and starts jogging over to me. "Hi Eoz, what's up?"

"Just checking in." I think she knows I'm asking her how she's feeling about Sciprus, because her smile disappears and she nods slowly.

"Well, I'm just trying to keep myself busy." She gestures to her bow.

"That's good. I guess I'll see you at dinner then," I reply.

I start to walk away, but Eilsel yells, "Wait!"

I turn around. "What?"

Eilsel's grin reappears. "Meet me in the woods tonight, I need to show you something."

"Okay, I'll see you there."

I leave Eilsel to be with the other archers. She continues to shoot at their targets and have a good time. Unfortunately, not everyone was having as much fun as she is.

The air starts to get cold and windy. Only minutes later the rain starts drizzling down on us. I go back to my tent to grab a coat, but instead I find Wren sitting on her cot holding a crumpled up piece of parchment.

As I approach her, I can see the black circles around her eyes.

"I miss him too," I say with sympathy as I sit down.

I can tell she's holding back tears.

"We never cry," Wren told me last night, yet it feels like ages ago.

She told me that commanders couldn't be scared, they had to be strong and confident. Thinking about her words now, they don't seem entirely true. However, I believed her and instantly stopped crying and held back the rest of my tears. I tried to keep it together after that.

Wren held my hand. "He was like a brother to me," she said after a moment.

"I know, but he would be proud of you—very, very proud." Wren lets a tear run down her cheek.

"Eoz, can I tell you a story?" she asks.

I nod. "Yeah, go ahead."

Wren fidgets with the parchment in her hand and finally starts. "A while ago, back when we still lived with our families, Sciprus and I would escape to a nearby swamp, quite similar to this one."

She gestures to the door of the tent. "Every day after school we would go to a swamp that was hidden behind many rocks and bushes, so most people didn't even know it existed."

She takes a breath and more tears ran down her cheek.

"One day after school we went there, we were skipping stones and trying to see who could get the most skips. I went first, on my first try, I only got two skips. Sciprus then got five skips. When it was his turn again, he reached for a stone that was perched on a tree stump about two yards away from him. He stepped toward the log to grab the stone, but he slipped on a piece of moss and tumbled into the water."

Now the tears really start to roll down her face, but she keeps going.

"Neither of us were good swimmers, so we never swam in the swamp. Sciprus kept rolling until he was completely underwater. I didn't know what to do. At first I thought he would bob right up like the ducks, but after a few moments passed I realized he was probably drowning. I started crying, I felt so helpless and feeble. I knew I couldn't dive in and save him. It felt like my throat was closing up, it felt like I was drowning right there with him. I did the only thing I could think of—I screamed for help.

"Shortly after, a man appeared from the bushes. He was wearing a fisherman's outfit and he held a fishing rod. I told him that Sciprus was in the swamp drowning and he had been under for a minute or so. The man dropped his pole and dove into the swamp. The man got Sciprus out Of the water and pumped all of the water out of him. The man told me that Sciprus' tunic got caught on a rock underwater, so he couldn't come to the surface. We were so lucky that the man had been at the swamp fishing otherwise Sciprus wouldn't have survived."

Wren puts her parchment in her pocket and wipes tears from her eyes.

"Wren, I'm so sorry, that's horrible," I say, squeezing her hand.

"I don't really remember what had happened after that, but I do know that that was the last time we went to that swamp," Wren tells me.

I nod, picturing Wren's young self crying and screaming because Sciprus was drowning in a swamp. I can picture her red face and knees shaking. I can't imagine what it would be like if Eilsel was drowning and I couldn't do anything to help.

"I'm so sorry," I say again.

This time Wren looks me right in the eye. "Eoz, I thought I lost him that day. I thought that was the end. So yesterday, when he took the arrow for me, I felt the same drowning feeling from all those years ago. I knew it should have been me who died, not him."

We sit in silence for a few minutes. The only sounds are the pitter patter of the rain drops falling against the canvas roof of our tent and the faint talking of other soldiers around the campground. Wren's story got me thinking about my relationship with Sciprus. I have only known him since the Starlight Festival, but it feels like he has been my friend forever. It seems like I have lived more life in the last three weeks than in the last twelve years. I'm not sure who to thank for that. Is it because of the war? Sciprus and Wren? Flares and Aurorans? I guess I'll never know for sure.

"Commander, someone is here to see you." A familiar voice comes from behind me.

"Abhey?"

Abhey leads me off the log and back into the campsite.

"What is it?" I ask impatiently.

He points over at a man with a scruffy beard and hazel eyes. He doesn't have any animal characteristics. He looks almost human.

"What does he want?" I question.

"I'm not sure. He just asked for Eilsel and Eoz Pawzord."

"Okay," I say, eyeing him suspiciously. "But let me grab my sword just in case."

Eilsel and I are standing so close together I can hear her heart beating with anticipation.

"Care to explain who you are?" I ask the man.

He sighs. "I'm Lachlan. Your, well, your father."

Eilsel gasps, and then glares. "I'm sorry. Am I hearing you right?"

"Yes, I am your father. I did ditch you and your mom when you two were born." He gulps. "And yes I was the one who created this war."

I lift my sword. "So, why did you decide to show up twelve years later to check in a war that you started?"

Eilsel kicks a rock around. I can tell she's nervous, which makes me raise my sword higher.

"Why do you show up now?" I insist.

"I'm on my way to Smitstown and I saw your training camp. I thought I would stop by."

I can't believe my ears. Fathers that completely turn on their families and reappear twelve years later and expect forgiveness? Oh, and that's another thing. Is he trying to apologize? I want to yell at him and tell him how terrible he is, but something is stopping me.

What if he actually is trying to apologize, what if he regrets leaving us and starting a war? I shake the thought out of my head and turn to Eilsel who is still kicking that rock around.

"Well, it's been nice meeting you," Eilsel says with an edge to her voice.

"Yes," I agree. "But you better be on your way. You'll want to arrive in Smitstown at a reasonable hour."

My twin and I exchange a look that's meant to say, 'Get this guy out of here now.'

Lachlan clears his throat, "Well, it is getting late. I suppose I should get going."

I nod. "Goodbye."

Eilsel doesn't look up, she just slides her foot around the rock until our father is out of sight.

"I'm leaving!" Wren says.

At first I don't even hear her. I was so alarmed by the appearance of my father that I can't think about anything else.

"What?" I ask, when I realize she's waiting for an answer.

"I'm leaving. I'm going to start the Mage rebellion! Of course, to remember Sciprus."

I shake my head trying to comprehend what has happened in the last five minutes. Everything is happening too fast.

"But you can't go! Will we ever see you again?" Eilsel whines.

"Of course you will. Meet me back in Scalia!" she says.

We give each other awkward hugs, trying to savor the last moments.

"Goodbye, Wren!" I call.

Before long, it's just the two of us.

"I still can't believe that's our dad," Eilsel says as we sit in my tent together.

"I know. I wouldn't expect him to show up." I reply. "Maybe Sciprus and Wren are right. Maybe he is a good guy."

EPILOGUE

The rain had been drizzling upon the soldiers' heads for many long hours, yet they continued marching. The Auroran-Flares had just suffered a devastating defeat at the hands of Commander Pawzord and her troops, so the morale was low. Bruises and cuts stung in the rain, which made it difficult for the soldiers to move quickly. Several people's uniforms were stained with color, due to a group of Scalian archers led by an unknown human child, and some even swore they saw incredibly strange things whenever they came into contact with a girl described as 'brown-haired and green-eyed.'

EPILOGUE

Very few people were unharmed, and even though they were further away from the battlefield, bodies were still strewn about across the ridge they just climbed. Most had died from their wounds, but others had contracted hypothermia because of the intense cold.

Hawken eyed his cousins walking along at the front of the pack. There were dark circles under their eyes, and even though he knew they didn't participate in the Battle of Colorful Snow the two looked utterly worn and defeated.

Despite his predicament, Red's eyes lit up when he saw Hawken. Agni looked even worse, if possible. Hawken pulled off his hood so Agni's troops would recognize him, his fiery orange hair marking him as a Flare. Hawken's eyes were so dark that they looked almost black, and they seemed to bore into Agni's soul. On the prophesied hero's belt rested a war axe that he was known for—he never went anywhere without it. He wore orange armor instead of the light blue that his cousins had been forced to wear, and he had brought extra for Red, his favorite of the two.

"We have been defeated," Agni told his cousin.

"I know. As expected—you are only fourteen," Hawken said coldly.

"I actually turned fifteen quite a while ago," Agni objected.

"It's all the same to me. You are but a pawn in this war—until you can prove otherwise, which I doubt will ever happen," Hawken quipped.

"Now, where is Red?" the oldest cousin said brightly.

Red, who had been standing idly at Agni's side, looked up and cheered, breaking the serious mood. "Right here! I have so, so, so much to tell you!"

"Come on, we will make camp here. I'm sure your older brother is at *least* competent enough to get it set up while you tell me all that has happened," Hawken commanded.

The rest of the soldiers put up their own tents near the three cousins' tents, but they were required to be out of earshot in case their general and commander talked about something confidential.

While Agni ordered the remaining soldiers to put up the tents, Red and Hawken sat down on a log.

"Go ahead, Red," Hawken prompted.

The boy took this as an all-clear to unleash an incredibly verbose stream of speech. "We were supposed to look for Fantasticals and maybe they're not so bad, but I haven't met them so I don't know and—"

"Slow down, Red," Hawken said.

"Sorry. We didn't find any Fantasticals, even though they were apparently seen by some principal guy in Starlight. We caught a Scalian soldier, though! But then he got away, so that wasn't great. Then Agni was all fancy and so boring because we had to prepare for battle with the Scalians. We didn't actually go, 'cause we're underage, but it was okay because something exciting happened while the others were fighting."

Hawken looked at Red quizzically. "Continue."

Red looked down at his feet sheepishly, as if realizing he'd messed up. "Actually, it's not very exciting... but I want to know about you! What did you do? It must be so much more interesting than what we did."

Hawken smiled in a way some would call sinister. "I captured a very valuable person to the enemy."

"Who? Have they told you anything helpful?" Red asked frantically.

"The only thing he told me was his name," Hawken replied.

"What is it?" Red wondered aloud.

"His name... is Aikai."

ACKNOWLEDGEMENTS

Firstly, a major thank you to our parents for everything. You pushed us to get our first draft done when we procrastinated, and we wouldn't even be writing a novel if it weren't for your support! ☺

Additionally, Ms. Smit, in the third grade you inspired us to write our first longer book. We didn't finish it, but that's where Eilsel and Eoz draw their names from. Thank you so much for all that you do, and anyone that has you as a teacher is a very lucky person!

Safiya, thank you so much for drawing our cover! We would have a cover-less book if it weren't for you, so thanks a million! Also, you were technically our first reader, so thanks for that as well! (Additionally, thank you to all of our friends for the support we received! You too, Mrs. Belenson.)

Kelly, Sonja, and Naomi, thank you for the guidance and wisdom that helped us to write and market our book. We couldn't have finished it without you!

Finally, to all of the teachers who taught us, thank you for your education. It would've been impossible to write a book without knowing how to read, after all! (Especially Ms. Madsen, Ms. G, and Ms. Casey, for expanding our vocabulary and teaching us grammar!)

ABOUT THE AUTHORS

Leslie Rosoff recently completed sixth grade in San Francisco, California. Her favorite animal is a shark, and her friends will tell you that she is mildly obsessed with them. Leslie loves to read as many books as she can get her hands on, which is a major inspiration to her writing today, as well as playing basketball, video games, and hanging out with friends and family.

Zoë Gilbertson loves to play volleyball, read fantasy and contemporary fiction novels, and spend time with her friends and family. She lives in San Francisco, California with her parents, brother, and sister. She spends much of her free time writing with her friend Leslie and by herself. Volleyball, friends, and day-to-day life act as important inspirations for her own writing.

CPSIA information can be obtained
at www.ICGtesting.com
Printed in the USA
BVHW042246230921
617409BV00016B/861